"What a pretty package," Evan teased Holly, who'd ended up a prisoner in the game she'd been playing with her best friend's son. "All tied up under my apple tree."

As he reached to stroke her jaw with his knuckles, Holly turned her head, but not so much as to break the tantalizing connection with his fingers.

He leaned over and kissed her neck. Twice. Slowly. "I love the way your hair smells," he murmured.

"Evan," Holly whispered, embarrassed. "Please don't do that."

"How about if I do this?" He kissed her on the mouth. Softly.

She drew a deep breath as sensations raced through her body at an alarming speed. "I don't think that's such a good idea either."

"Oh, but I think it's a wonderful idea. In fact"—he paused to kiss her again—"I think you like it too."

Holly swallowed. It was hard to think while he stroked her face. "You're taking advantage of me, Evan. You shouldn't—" She stopped talking when his lips brushed hers again. "You—" she tried again, then surrendered to the desire he'd awakened in her. There was no turning back now. . . .

WHAT ARE *LOVESWEPT* ROMANCES?

They are stories of true romance and touching emotion. We believe those two very important ingredients are constants in our highly sensual and very believable stories in the *LOVESWEPT* line. Our goal is to give you, the reader, stories of consistently high quality that may sometimes make you laugh, sometimes make you cry, but are always fresh and creative and contain many delightful surprises within their pages.

Most romance fans read an enormous number of books. Those they truly love, they keep. Others may be traded with friends and soon forgotten. We hope that each *LOVESWEPT* romance will be a treasure—a "keeper." We will always try to publish

LOVE STORIES YOU'LL NEVER FORGET
BY AUTHORS YOU'LL ALWAYS REMEMBER

The Editors

Loveswept ®543

Susan Connell
Glory Girl

BANTAM BOOKS
NEW YORK · TORONTO · LONDON · SYDNEY · AUCKLAND

GLORY GIRL

A Bantam Book / May 1992

If you would be interested in receiving protective vinyl
covers for your Loveswept books, please write to this address
for information:

Loveswept
Bantam Books
P.O. Box 985
Hicksville, NY 11802

ISBN 0-553-44240-6

Published simultaneously in the United States and Canada

PRINTED IN THE UNITED STATES OF AMERICA

OPM   0 9 8 7 6 5 4 3 2 1

For the Waldenettes: Kathy, Linda, and Denise

One

"My daddy's got your red pichure."

Holly Hamilton's fingers stiffened in the sand. Only one thing mattered. Anonymity. And she'd just lost it.

In a singsong voice the child who had materialized beside Holly's beach towel continued, "You still don't got your panties on." High-pitched giggling accompanied by a great deal of jumping up and down followed.

Holly tugged at her swimsuit, then pushed herself up into a sitting position. Heads were already turning in their direction as she pulled the brim of her straw hat to the bridge of her nose. "Does your mama know where you are?" she whispered through clenched teeth.

Oblivious to Holly's question, the child continued loudly, "I'm gonna tell my daddy. I am. And my uncle Teddy. He's got your red pichure too."

Holly began struggling into her caftan, determined to put a premature end to her afternoon on the beach. She'd specifically chosen the isolated and normally less crowded Dune Island Beach over one closer to her cottage. She'd been so careful, so discreet . . . so stupid to venture out. Holly jerked the hood over her head and readjusted her sunglasses and hat just as the child's mother arrived.

"Katie! Here you are. You scared me half to death."

The mother grabbed the child by the elbow and began leading her away. "Haven't I told you never to talk to strangers?"

"But Mommy—" the child protested.

Holly quickly scanned the beach to see who might have overheard. The good-looking man she'd been peeking at shifted lower in his beach chair. Maybe he hadn't heard. Maybe that smile underneath his sunglasses had nothing to do with him recognizing her. She took a shallow breath and held it. Several prickling seconds later she released it. "Maybe" wasn't good enough.

ESCAPE blinked in Holly's mind's eye like a throbbing neon sign. When would this all end? It had been over a year since she'd left modeling. Over a year since she'd finally decided what she really wanted to do with her life. And now celebrity had reared its unwelcome head again! Shoving the rest of her possessions into her tote, she looked toward the path leading back to the changing pavilion. Three college-age young men singing the Morning Glory Soap jingle were heading straight toward her. *My God,* she thought, *they're coming at me from all directions.*

"I'm telling you, Dougie. Older women. Take the Glory Girl . . ." one of the young men began.

Momentary silence. Then, in unison, the three young men yowled lustily.

Holly froze at the mention of the Glory Girl. Things couldn't get any worse . . . unless the handsome stranger had heard, confirming his possible suspicions about who was hiding behind the dark glasses and hat. She chanced a look in his direction. He hadn't moved one muscle of his gorgeous body, but the college trio was moving closer and getting louder. She cringed at the next remark.

"Tush. Pure and simple. Ah, what a piece!"

"Nah. It's that surprised look in her eyes. They say her husband took the photo without her permission, and since their divorce he's been making a fortune from the posters. The man's a genius, I mean, putting it out in three colors. Which one did you get, Dougie?"

Dougie pressed the palms of his hands together and, in an attitude of prayer, dropped to his knees in the sand. "The gold one."

Hearing their every word, Holly's hands tightened along the edge of her hat brim. Stuart Hamilton, ex-husband and rat, was going to pay for all this humiliation. But first she had to escape from Dune Island State Park and make it back to the Cape Shell beach house. Then she had to call her lawyer to find out if capital punishment was yet in effect in New York. Maybe murdering Stu wasn't such a crazy idea after all. Grabbing her tote and her towel, she made a dash for the path.

Evan Jamieson dropped his head back against his chair with an exasperated sigh. "Gone," he whispered to a perplexed-looking sea gull strutting nearby.

Probably the best body he'd ever seen had just left, and he'd never even got a good look at her face. In a flurry of turquoise, she'd hightailed it off the beach like a whirling dervish, her hand firmly planted on top of that damn hat! Because of it and those sunglasses he could only imagine her face.

He'd been keeping an eye—correction, both eyes—on that one-piece orange suit. Lying there at his feet . . . well, ten yards away anyway, playing peekaboo with him. The scenario had a vaguely familiar feel to it. Had they played this game together somewhere in his fantasies? He squirmed in his chair as he pictured her reaching to adjust the hat. A fragment of memory teased at his consciousness. Where had he seen her before? Her suit, already cut to the hip bones, rode higher still, revealing creamy white flesh above her tan line. The orange suit, the light tan on her legs, and the cream-white line at her hip . . . He thought of a good old-fashioned Creamsicle, and his mouth began to water. He looked past the college kids already spreading out to take her place and toward the path leading to the pavilion and the parking lot.

Evan drummed his fingers against the arms of his chair. Here he was, thinking about Creamsicles, while she was getting away. He did need a vacation! He stood up, startling the sea gull into flight as he collapsed his beach chair and threw his shirt onto his shoulder. Sprinting toward the pavilion, he remembered the words of his flight surgeon, the words that convinced him to use the beach house for the month of August.

"Rest, exercise, unwind a little. Have some fun, Ev. You're in great shape. Let's keep it that way." With the sand gritting beneath his feet, Evan Jamieson agreed with gusto. "Roger that, Doc." Now, if he could catch up with her . . .

Leaning against the stall in the bathroom, Holly dug through the contents of her tote again. Her keys weren't there. She swore under her breath at her carelessness. Somewhere between the beach and the pavilion she'd lost the car keys, and she couldn't risk returning to the beach area to search for them. Not with old Dougie and his friends out there drooling over the Glory Girl.

She looked down at the thin sandals she'd dumped on the floor, slipped her feet into them, and sighed with resignation. She wasn't looking forward to a seven-mile walk back to Cape Shell, but there was no other alternative. Calling a service station would lead to bullet-speed publicity. Calling the local cab company would probably take forever. The one person in Cape Shell who knew her situation and could help her would be up to her elbows in Italian dressing and imported salami right about now. Annie's Deli must be in high gear with the late-afternoon crowd, and would be for quite some time.

Holly opened the stall door a crack and looked out. She couldn't stay in here forever. Knowing she'd have to forgo the cold drinks at the crowded refreshment stand, she stealthily made her way toward the bank of water fountains. The water turned out to be low pressure and lukewarm, but she gulped it down. It was going to be a long walk back.

"A bad day at the beach is better than a good day at work," someone had once told her. Well, she'd had quite a day at the beach so far. She'd managed to delight one beautiful child, send three young males into rut, and humiliate herself in front of *him.* And now she was preparing to walk seven hot, dusty miles in the thinnest sandals she owned. She began lifting her head from the fountain, ready to laugh at the absurdity of her situation. Halfway up she heard someone humming the Morning Glory Soap jingle. She stopped suddenly, not daring to lift her head a fraction of an inch more. The young man from the beach—Dougie—had entered the pavilion.

Without hesitating, Holly turned from the sound and ran smack into a very broad, very masculine set of pectorals. A beach chair, the tote bag, and Holly's sunglasses clattered to the cement floor. Quickly followed by an ice-cream bar still in its wrapper.

Glancing nervously over her shoulder, Holly knelt down and fished her glasses from the pile. She pushed them on. "I apologize, I really do," she whispered to the pair of feet before her. Darting glances over her shoulder, she managed to pick up the dropped items and shove them into a large pair of hands. This day at the beach was turning into a nightmare. She reached for the ice-cream bar, noting almost unconsciously that it was a Creamsicle.

"Excuse me? Are you okay?" The voice was deep and steady, sending a slight shock wave of feminine awareness through her. "Are you in some kind of trouble?"

"What? No, no, of course not." Holly tugged at her hat brim, bringing it close to one cheek. "Here." She dropped the paper-wrapped ice cream into his hand and froze. It couldn't be. Not the stranger across the beach with the shoulders to kill for and a smile that . . . She let go of her hat brim and stared up at him.

"I thought I recognized you from—" he began as she stood.

"No," she began firmly before he could say it. "I'm not who you think I am. You're wrong." And, as an afterthought, "I'm sorry."

She scurried past the refreshment stand, then out through the closest exit before realizing she was exiting south and away from Cape Shell. With sand hitting the backs of her legs, she hurried along the south wall. Someone was following her. Breaking into a run, she rounded the corner of the cinder-block structure and skidded on macadam. A steadying hand closed around her wrist, saving her from a fall.

"Excuse me?"

There it was again. That voice that sent shivers to the pit of her stomach. Holly's shoulders sagged. *Please God, don't let him be a reporter,* she prayed. She turned warily around to face him. "Yes?"

He handed her the tote she had tossed into his hands moments before. "Thanks anyway, but I really think you want this back."

"My bag!" She took it with both hands and clutched it to her chest. Her address book, her credit cards, her driver's license . . . her name. "Thank you."

"By the way, you're getting quite a sunburn on that nose, and I do recognize you from the beach today." He tore the bottom out of the ice-cream wrapper. "If I'm not mistaken," he said, knowing full well he wasn't, "there's an orange bathing suit underneath your, uh . . ." He pointed with the dripping ice cream.

Before Holly could say "caftan," he'd pulled the ice cream from its wrapper and bit off a good-size chunk. She watched his cheeks hollow in and his lips purse as he sucked on the mouthful. She wasn't sure how he managed it, but he looked damn sexy eating a dripping Creamsicle.

"That was me on the beach," she mumbled as he took another huge bite. He didn't act like any reporter she'd ever met. Reporters tended to hold microphones, not ice cream, and their shouted questions came swiftly and with barbs.

The stranger's lips remained brazenly pursed for the longest time. He nodded finally, then walked past her. Was it possible? she wondered, turning to watch him. Hadn't he recognized the Glory Girl?

A short distance away he was busy opening the trunk of his Mercedes. Tossing in his beach chair, he pulled out a pair of brown leather boating shoes. Looking in her direction and smiling, he tilted his head to a questioning angle. Ah, here it comes, she thought, the polite request for an autograph. She waited. But the request didn't come.

She watched him closely and wondered vaguely if he was staring back while his tongue lavished attention on the dripping ice cream. With a thoroughness that sent quivers through her body, he thrust all but the end of the stick into his mouth, then slowly drew it out. Then he did it again. As his tongue slipped under the remaining lump, she flicked her tongue over her lips. And when he finally stroked off the last bit of cream with the tip of his tongue, she swallowed hard.

His lips glistened as he spoke. "Thought I had a meltdown going there for a moment."

Meltdown? She hadn't watched a man's mouth do anything like that since . . . come to think of it, in all her twenty-seven years she'd never seen anyone do that before. She blinked. The sun had become unbearably hot on her skin, making her temples ache. Yes, that was it. The sun was to blame for the crazy pictures in her mind and the resulting sensations pulsating through her body. Recapturing her composure, she forced a shrug. "Gotta watch those meltdowns," she offered with an airy innocence she didn't feel.

He moved his head to one side again. "Are you sure everything's okay?"

He didn't recognize her. For a moment relief washed over her, and then the oddest thing happened. A slight but definite feeling of disappointment seeped in. She was dumbfounded at her own reaction, because disappointment was the last thing she should be feeling after all she'd gone through to protect her identity. "I lost my car keys."

"Hmmm." He dropped his shoes to the pavement and stepped into them. "Where do you think you lost them?"

"Probably the beach. I only realized I'd lost them a moment before I ran into you at the fountain," she said, remembering how she'd bolted from him in the pavilion.

"Right," he agreed with an understanding nod. "Why don't you look in the pavilion, and I'll check back on the beach? By the way, what do they look like?"

Holly toyed with the side of her sunglasses as feelings of anxiousness started again. If he wasn't a reporter, why was he offering to help her? He didn't even know her. She winced. She was so tired of suspicion and mistrust. Where would it all end?

The stranger stepped closer, offering her his hand. "I'm sorry. I haven't introduced myself. I'm Evan Jamieson. And you are . . . ?"

"H-Hilary Smith," she lied, allowing him to take her hand.

Ordinarily, she made a point of looking into the eyes of the person she was shaking hands with, but Evan Jamieson was still wearing his sunglasses. She found her stare fixated on the chiseled planes of his mouth and the slight sheen left there by the ice cream. His grip was strong, yet gentle, and he held her hand a few seconds longer than necessary. Holly's heart thumped with a combination of excitement and fear. Who was Evan Jamieson, and why was shaking hands with him so extraordinarily . . . intimate? A few grains of sand were trapped between their fingers, heightening further her tactile awareness of him. She quickly pulled her hand from his and took a step backward.

"My keys? Oh, yes, they're on a bamboo ring with a little plastic lemon hanging from it."

He shrugged into his shirt. "Ten minutes?"

Rubbing her palms together, she felt the grains of sand, and it was as if he was touching her again. She nodded, and only then did he turn to go. Madras button downs never looked so good, she decided, watching him break into a trot across the parking lot. When he disappeared behind the dune, she dashed off to the bathroom to hide until he returned.

Ten minutes later Holly was back by his car watching him cross the parking lot.

"Have any luck in the pavilion?"

She took a step away from the car and shook her head guiltily. He'd been out on that hot sand searching for her keys while she'd been hiding in a cool, shadowy building. "No, but Mr. Jamieson, thank you so much for looking. I really appreciate it."

He held up his hand. "Evan, please. What are you going to do now?"

She shrugged. "Start walking."

He pulled back in mock horror. "You weren't. Not in those," he said, pointing to her sandals.

Holly looked down and wriggled her toes. The sandals' thin straps and delicate beading didn't appear sturdy enough to cross a carpeted living room, let alone a designated wilderness area.

She grinned sheepishly. "Afraid so."

He shook his head. "You won't last a mile in those things. Why don't you let me drive you back?" He watched her hesitate. Nice to know she's cautious, he thought, but that wasn't helping either of them at the moment. He unlocked the passenger door. "Your mother was right most of the time."

She backed away. "About what?"

"About not taking rides from strangers." He watched as she looked him over once again. "For what it's worth, you'll be perfectly safe with me."

Common sense fought with feminine instinct. He'd been more than generous with his time, and he did appear to be sincere. And well balanced. She laughed softly at the last thought. Living in New York as long as she had, she'd developed a sixth sense about people. Evan Jamieson felt safe. Any lingering uneasiness was natural, considering her present circumstances. "Well, if you promise never to tell my mother . . ." she began teasingly.

"If you promise never to tell mine," he said, pulling open the door.

The interior was stiflingly hot, but Holly let out a grateful sigh once she was inside. She'd been lingering in a public place much too long. The sooner she disappeared from view, the better. Holly smiled at Evan, then reached out and pulled the door shut.

Evan walked around his car, lifted the trunk, and then shut it before he opened his door and slid into the driver's seat. "Sorry I took so long," he said as he placed his paper on the dashboard, started the car, and turned on the air conditioner. "You're in a hurry, I take it?"

Holly removed her hat and wiped the perspiration from her forehead. "Me? In a hurry? What makes you ask that?"

Evan shrugged as a quirky smile tugged at his mouth.

She allowed him to take her hat and toss it on the backseat. His right arm came to rest on the back of her seat, and for a moment he said nothing. Then he lifted his sunglasses to the top of his head, and Holly found herself staring into a pair of deep-blue eyes shining with intelligence, wit, and questions.

"My windows are tinted, so you can take off your sunglasses."

She started to remove them, then hastily slipped them back on. Her glasses were the last barrier to Evan's full-face view of the Glory Girl. Sooner or later he'd find out the truth, but right now later seemed so much better. "They're prescription."

"But how will I ever see the color of your eyes?" he asked with feigned innocence.

"They're green," she explained with business-like efficiency as she adjusted her seat belt. When she turned back to him, she saw his eyes narrowing to skeptical slits. If she wasn't careful, she'd arouse his suspicion. She smiled calmly. "Really, they're light green. My dad says they look like anemic shamrocks."

"You're a very mysterious lady, Miss Hilary Smith. Tell me more about yourself. Like what you do when you're not dealing with traumatic childhood events like that?"

She would have loved to explain her father's sense of humor, but she hardly knew Evan. She also wanted to scold him for treating the subject of childhood trauma so lightly, though somehow she knew he was the kind of person who wouldn't. "I'm a travel writer," she lied. "I, uh, freelance. How about you?"

"Aircraft management. Corporate and private. And I occasionally pilot a plane myself."

Tucking her legs under her, she turned toward

him. "Isn't that the kind of business where you fly the rich and famous around?"

"The rich, but usually not so famous."

Holly nodded. The thing to do now was to keep the conversation away from her. Besides, his job did sound interesting. "Well, where do you fly?"

"All over. I've been in South America for the last four months. Mostly Peru." The air conditioner had finally blown most of the hot air from the car, and he pulled his door shut. "It's good to be back." He shifted into drive then turned to her with a thoughtful smile. "It's a pleasure to meet you, Hilary."

No one had ever smiled at her in quite the way he was smiling now. Or, if anyone had, she'd never before experienced such an immediate and intensely visceral response. There was a challenge in the depths of his eyes, and it seemed to say "If you'll allow it, we're going to have a wonderful time." His sensual energy continued rippling through her like a fresh breeze on a hot afternoon, eroding her doubt. She relaxed against the seat, almost giddy with the knowledge that she remained incognito.

"It's a pleasure meeting you, too, Evan. Thanks again for looking for my car keys and for offering to drive me back. I'm staying just across the bridge in Cape Shell."

"Me too."

"Vacation?"

Nodding, he swung his car out of the parking lot and headed toward the bridge at the north end of Dune Island State Park. "Flight surgeon told me it was time to work on my tan. Maybe build a few sand castles and meet Hilary Smith." He glanced at her. "Seriously, our flight surgeon gets a bit cranky if we let three years go by without taking a vacation. And you?"

"Me? Just a vacation."

Ah, Hilary Smith, he thought. What a beautiful woman. What a terrible liar. What an intriguing combination.

Anxious to change the subject, she continued quickly, "You mentioned Peru before. Were you there during the earthquake?"

"Yes." He glanced across the car's interior and caught her checking the rearview mirror. She was still skittish about accepting a ride from him. She was definitely running from something on the beach, too, and she was avoiding talking about herself. What did he have here? What was she really? A mob moll on the run? A beauty pursued by a jealous lover? Could she be hiding from a blackmailer? Well, he wouldn't push. Patience, he told himself. Patience always paid. He decided to let her have the next words, whenever she was ready. What a looker she was. What he could see of her, that is. She wore those glasses like a piece of armor. What kind of fire-breathing dragon was threatening her anyway? Who or what would force her to walk back to town in this hellish heat? Patience, patience, he counseled himself.

Evan looked out the window to gather his thoughts. This crazy speculating wasn't like him at all, but she could be trudging along the roadside right now, perhaps carrying a sandal or two with broken straps. The beauty of wild beach plum and other scrubby vegetation couldn't cancel out his thoughts. She might never have made it back. She could've succumbed to heat prostration. Or God knows what.

"Well, aren't you going to tell me about it?" she asked, interrupting his thoughts.

Heat prostration? Circling buzzards? "About what?"

"The earthquake. What was it like?"

"It scared the hell out of me. We were in Cuzco, and half my hotel was turned into rubble."

"Were you hurt?"

"No, but the shoe-shine boy in the lobby broke his leg. Luckily the airport was operational. We flew him down to Lima. You know, the kid had never been in an airplane before. The ride inside a luxury jet coupled with the painkillers had him believing he was on his way to heaven." Evan shook his head. "Makes you realize how lucky you are when something like that happens."

Holly nodded. "What happened to him?"

"We had a fax last week from my client. The boy's healing nicely and wants to go flying again."

Holly laughed along with Evan. "You know, that was a wonderful thing you did. Helping out like that. Children are so helpless during a disaster. I wish more people were like you."

She was relaxing. He meant to keep her that way too. "Sounds like you have a special interest in this sort of thing."

"I do volunteer work for Lemon Aid. It's a disaster-relief organization." She became more animated as she continued. "It's children helping children on a grass-roots level. They hold car washes, walk dogs, clean out garages, stuff like that. The money they raise goes to relief efforts for other children, who are caught up in disasters."

"No kidding. Sounds worthwhile. What exactly do you do?"

Holly sank back in her seat and dutifully retested her seat-belt buckle. This man was too easy to talk to. She'd really have to watch what she was saying. "I just help out licking stamps, stuffing envelopes. That's all. Tell me more about your stay in Peru."

By the time they'd driven up and parked by a small strip of stores in Cape Shell, he had her laughing about some timid llamas he'd happened upon in some ancient Incan ruins.

"I need a few things in here. Want to come in with me?"

She was about to say yes, but when Holly glanced out her window, reality took hold again. Too many people. Too many chances to be recognized. "That's okay. I'll just wait here."

Watching him saunter into the little grocery store, she felt a wave of depression weigh down on her. What would he do if someone recognized her while they were together? She remembered the mob scene on Madison Avenue last week. What would he think if he knew about a poster of her naked backside going for ten dollars a shot? She winced. Whoever said life was fair was probably the same jerk who promised that marriage was forever.

Evan returned a few minutes later with two paper sacks and put them on the backseat. He raised his chin in the direction of one of the sacks. "I've got to get to my freezer pronto. Mind if I drop this frozen stuff at my house?"

Another few minutes with him? "I don't mind."

"Good. Then we'll call a dealership to see about a replacement key."

Holly shoved a lock of hair behind her ear and grinned. Evan's energy filled the car, leaving little room for depressing thoughts. "You think of everything. Are you always so good at solving problems for strangers?"

Evan laughed. "Actually, that's exactly what I do at my office—smooth out rough spots for our clients. But enough about work. This is my vacation." He looked at the larger brown sack. "There's a present for you in that one."

"Me?" she peered in and laughed. Lifting out the plastic tube, she read the front of it. "Zinc Ointment. You didn't have to buy me this."

"Nonsense. Someone had to. That nose is bright enough to put Rudolph out of work."

During her modeling days she'd used enough sunblock to stock a chain of pharmacies. Today she'd forgotten to use any. Holly jerked down the windshield visor and leaned in toward the mirror attached to it. Groaning, she slapped the visor back into place. Because he'd leaned in to look, too, their faces were inches away from each other.

"I thought my hat was taking care . . . of . . . that problem."

"Is that right?" His voice was husky as he leaned a fraction of an inch closer. "Back there on the beach you kept readjusting that hat every time you looked my way."

Holly felt her mouth go dry. "I didn't know you . . ."

"Were looking back? I couldn't take my eyes off you." Evan reached to remove her sunglasses when someone began pounding on his window.

"Hey, buddy. Take her home and kiss her. I need this parking space for my deliveries."

Evan turned around to see a huge, grinning face, framed by two cupped hands, pressed against his side window.

A soft sibilant curse broke from Evan's lips, but he gave the man a smile and partial salute.

Shielding her face with one hand, Holly sank low in her seat. This was not that bad, she told herself. Certainly not as bad as that one reporter, Dennis Cracci, following her into the ladies' room with a microphone. All the same, she found herself crouching lower.

She watched Evan look into his side mirror and shift gears. With good-natured restraint he looked over his shoulder and commented, "I don't think I want to cross the Hulk. His truck looks pretty big."

"No," Holly agreed. "You don't want to cross the Hulk." That's all she needed, involvement in an altercation with a burly truck driver and a gorgeous man like Evan. Wouldn't the press just love it!

She kept her head down as they drove along the crowded street. In a surprisingly short time Evan was reaching for the remote-control garage-door opener on the console. "We're home. And I can't wait to hear why you're practically wedged under my dashboard."

She sat up and looked out the window. The paved drive to the three-story house was remarkably familiar, as was the six-foot privacy fence surrounding it. Her mouth fell open in genuine surprise. "Is this a joke? I mean, you've got to be kidding."

Evan drove inside the garage and aimed the control over his shoulder. "Hilary, you're evading the issue." The door clamored shut. "Do you usually ride in the fetal position, or is it my driving?"

"Evan," she began, ignoring his question, "I'm in the house directly behind this one. Right behind you. The little house," she added, as if he hadn't heard her.

"Annie rented that out, did she?" His eyebrows moved closer together and then, suddenly, apart. An easy grin slid across his face. "This is going to be a very interesting vacation," he said, reaching for his pager and clipping it to his waistband.

Holly smiled warily and shook her head. "Wait a minute. This is too much of a coincidence." But she'd known Annie since junior high, and Annie wouldn't do anything to screw things up for her. "It's just . . . Evan, this is—"

That slow, sure smile was lighting his face again. "I think, Hilary, they call it kismet," he offered, reaching for a sack of groceries. The devastating smile never quit. "What do you think?"

Kismet? She felt as if she'd been clinging to a rope and was suddenly asked to let go of it. To trust. She looked at the tube of zinc ointment still clutched in her hand, and then she looked at him. She should leave right now. She should say thank you very much, but no thank you, and be on her way. She really should. The silly yet practical gift had touched her, and so did the honesty she found in his eyes. Trust him? Maybe, just a little, for a while, she could. "Maybe."

"Maybe," he repeated, winking. "Then gather up your things and come on in."

She did, following him from the garage and into a spacious kitchen–dining room area. She stared up at the skylight and landing above the dining room. "This place is wonderful. You must have a very large family." She turned to face him. He wasn't wearing a wedding ring, but these days that was not necessarily a sign of bachelorhood.

He'd gone directly to the refrigerator and was stuffing the first sack into the freezer section. "Before you have to ask, the answer is no. I'm not married. This friendly old monster of a house is a hand-me-down from my folks. They moved to Florida three years ago."

A smile played on Evan's lips. He shut the freezer compartment, then shoved the second bag into the refrigerator.

Holly nodded solemnly, trying hard not to return his smile. She cleared her throat. "Do you always store your groceries like that?"

He shut the refrigerator door, then took her by the hand and drew her toward the wide central staircase. "Always when Hilary Smith comes to visit and remarks that my beach house is wonderful. Come on, I'll show you where I jumped off the landing using Uncle Carl's umbrella as my parachute. I was six at the time and watching too many cartoons."

Laughing, she allowed him to draw her up the stairs, then across the landing. Evan slapped the railing.

"This is where I began my career in aviation. Of course, my landings have shaped up considerably since then."

"Evan, you could have broken your neck."

"My leg, actually." Taking her hand he led her into a wide hallway. "I spent July and part of August of that year in here," he continued, pushing open the first door on the left. She hesitated. "Come on. You don't want to miss this point of interest on the tour. I promise, it's better than Graceland and the White House combined."

She followed him into the shadowed room. There was shared amusement in his eyes as he leaned her back against the wall. "This," he said smiling, "is a bedroom wall I hoped never to have to look at again."

Evan Jamieson studied the beauty before him. He reached up, took off her sunglasses, and dropped them to the carpet. It was too dark to see the color of her eyes, but they sparkled in the thin light coming in through the shuttered windows. He reached to touch her hair, which cascaded to her shoulders in silky waves of golden red. And her face . . . well, if she wasn't a model, she ought to be, he thought. Desire soared through him with the shocking speed of unsuspected wind shear. He forced his voice to remain casual, but he was fast losing that battle. "The Hulk said to take you home and kiss you."

Feeling recklessly happy, she reached up and placed her hands against his chest. She didn't want to think about the fear and uncertainties presently ruling her life. She only wanted this moment with this man and the feeling he stirred inside her. As wonderful and as real a feeling as she'd ever known. "Well, we don't want to cross the Hulk," she said, feigning surrender to a shared conspiracy, "because his truck is pretty big."

"No, not because of his truck, Hilary," Evan whispered, twisting his head to lower it to hers. "Just because."

His lips were warm as they brushed hers. Her eyelids fluttered closed, but not before she saw what hung on the opposite wall. "Oh my God!" Holly thumped him hard on both shoulders. "How could you!" She shoved him away with tightened fists.

"Ouch! What?"

Pointing across the room to the framed poster on the opposite wall, she growled her frustration. Then, her voice spilling over with hurt and accusation, she spoke. "You knew." She lowered her head, bouncing both her fists on her thighs as she did so. "You knew from the first moment you saw me, didn't you?"

"Knew what?" Evan looked genuinely confused.

"That I'm the Glory Girl."

Two

Evan squinted through the shadows behind him. A framed poster of a nude female caught his attention. The girl in the gold-tone poster was staring back over her shoulder. She appeared to be emerging from a musical instrument. Or was it a flower? Evan took a step closer.

Holly flicked on the light switch. "Go on. Get a good look. Everyone else has," she snapped.

He knew he should be looking at Hilary, but he couldn't help himself. He kept staring at the poster. The naked beauty with the strawberry-blonde hair fanning around her shoulders was emerging from a honey-colored morning glory. An unquestionable quality of candor dominated the composition. He noted the deliciously imperfect circle of her mouth and the glinting green of her eyes looking back over her shoulder. From the tilt of her right hip to the graceful way she was splaying her fingers on the velvety petal, the model had definitely been caught off guard. And she was mad as hell!

"Hilary? Is that—that *is* you!"

Holly picked up her sunglasses from where he'd dropped them, then shoved past him and out of the room. Hurrying out to the landing, she shouted, "Just how dumb do you think I am? How dare you trick me into trusting you when all you wanted was to get your hands on the Glory Girl!" Grabbing the top of the banister she twisted around and shouted even louder. "You were watching me on the beach all afternoon planning this whole thing. Go ahead, admit it!"

There was no answer. The slightest tremor of curiosity pulsed through her. Why wasn't he out in the hall apologizing or lying some more? What was he doing in there?

"Evan Jamieson, the least you can do is be man enough to answer me."

He did. The longest, loudest wolf whistle she'd ever heard cut through the silence. Lifting her chin, she drew on her pride and marched down the stairs. She'd actually allowed herself to think this Jamieson character could be someone special. "Kismet," he'd said. What a card-carrying romantic fool she was turning into. She snatched her belongings from the countertop and headed out the glass sliding doors. The little cottage across the brick patio never looked so inviting.

"Wait a minute. I remember you. *Sports Illustrated.* Green suede bikini on the beach in Mykonos." Evan stepped out of the bedroom. "Right?" The only answer was a door being shut. He crossed the landing to watch her from the back window. Her squared shoulders and determined stride would have made a perfect exit, except that she managed to trip over the garden hose on the way. He shoved the window open. "Hey, we have to talk."

Without responding, she reached the screened porch of her cottage and jerked the door open. A pronounced *bang* soon followed, and then another as she entered the cottage. Evan leaned both hands on the windowsill and smiled.

"Dinner in an hour, Hilary," he said quietly. She hadn't heard him. He hadn't meant for her to. Not yet, anyway.

Looking around his beach house, he welcomed the old memories as they rushed back in. He'd never sell the place, no matter what his accountants had recommended. One day, when he had children of his own . . . Allowing the unfinished thought to linger, he returned to the threshold of the guest room and stared at the poster again. The photo, candid as it appeared, was definitely the work of a professional photographer. The expert lighting, the morning-glory prop, and the perfection of Hilary—no one had skin that flawless— proved that.

What had she called herself? The Glory Girl? Well, the Glory Girl was more than a girl, she was all woman. What couldn't be seen could well be imagined. Evan cleared his throat, turned out the light, and shut the door. Poster art had come a long way since his college days.

Time for a shower. A cold shower, he amended, making his way to the master bedroom. Absolutely no one had skin like that.

Making a check-in call to Air Service International, he was informed his business had not dropped off the stock exchange since he'd left it last evening. None of ASI's testier clients had called to ask for him either. Contract renegotiations were about to begin with one, and Evan wanted them handled with kid gloves.

"This is your vacation, Mr. Jamieson. Please see to it that you enjoy it," Tally, his secretary, instructed him.

Evan glanced out his back bedroom window at the cottage. "I fully intend to, Tally. Call me, though, if—" He didn't bother to finish his sentence. Tally had hung up.

Stripping off his shirt and swim trunks, he reached into the linen closet and pulled out a towel and bar of soap. He started to tear the wrapper from the soap, and there she was again, the Glory Girl. Only this time the trumpet of petals was a rich pink and, compared to the poster, offered a very modest profile of her head and shoulders. Beneath the picture on the wrapper were the simple words *Morning Glory Soap, a glorious way to start your day . . . and end it.* He chuckled to himself as he headed toward the shower.

Showering quickly, he dressed in khaki shorts and a T-shirt, reattached his pager to his belt, then headed downstairs. He whistled a tune he'd heard but didn't know the name of. A tune that matched his mood perfectly. It was time to start the charcoal; he had a glorious evening planned.

Holly placed her writing pad and pencil on the floor of the screened porch, picked up her ice water, and continued swaying on the porch swing.

Concentrating on a fund-raising letter for Lemon Aid was next to impossible when the memory of Evan Jamieson's wolf whistle kept interrupting her thoughts. An extra flood of heat rushed to her sunburned face when she thought about how willing she'd been for his kiss. Eager, even.

She lifted her legs and stretched them across the wooden slats, placing her feet on the opposite arm rest. As soon as Annie got here with the groceries, Holly would discuss the possibilities of moving to another secluded rental. Fat chance, though, of finding a rental for August. She had lucked into this place several weeks ago only because she knew Annie. People had reserved Cape Shell houses as far back as last summer. It looked as if she might be stuck in Evan's back-yard. She pressed the plastic tumbler to her temple and blew at the irritating strands of hair sticking to her face. There was barely a breeze, and a land breeze at that, to move the hair that had slipped from her ponytail. Her gaze strayed to the sliding glass doors across the patio. One thing was for sure—she didn't want another heated exchange with Evan Jamieson.

As if on cue the sliding door opened, and out stepped Evan. Holly dropped a foot to the floor, stilling the swing. It was like seeing him for the first time all over again; she couldn't take her eyes off him. His hair was wet and slicked back, making it easy for her to remember how he'd looked emerging from the ocean. The crisp, dark hair dusting his body had glistened with ocean water. Shorts and a T-shirt now covered his tall, broad-shouldered body. His reddish-tan skin reminded her of a lifeguard she'd drooled over as a teenager.

One wet lock of hair fell over his forehead, and with casual precision Evan smoothed it back from his incredibly blue eyes—bluer now because of the heightened color of his face.

Mesmerized, she watched as he entered the storage shed next to his house. After a loud crash and several cuss words, he wheeled out a barbecue grill. In a few moments he'd filled it with a mound of charcoal, squirted the mound with starter fluid, then threw in a lighted match. And he didn't even bother to glance toward her cottage before he reentered his house. Not that it mattered to her, she reminded herself. She snatched up her pad and pencil, then leaned back and waited.

A short time later the slider opened again. Evan stepped outside with everything needed for a cookout piled high on a tray. Holly dropped the pad and pencil once again, and slowly sat up. She was never going to get the letter roughed out. And now what was he doing? Straining her neck, she saw him placing the tray on the table, opening the table's umbrella, then arranging plates and eating utensils. For two. Two? He had a dinner guest coming?

Both of Holly's feet hit the floor along with the plastic glass of ice water she'd been holding. He was walking toward her with a bottle of beer in each hand. She didn't know if the shiver she felt was from the icy splash from her tumbler, or from his presence. The last time Evan Jamieson was close, they'd almost kissed.

"Hello in there." He pressed his nose to the screened door. "Care to join me for a beer and some sparkling conversation? Dinner'll be ready in about half an hour, and you're invited."

"Dinner?"

His cheerful, confident tone continued. "Yes, you know. Comes between lunch and a midnight snack."

Ignoring her wet leg, she pushed herself up from the swing and walked casually toward him. "All this for an autograph, Jamieson?"

Laughing, he leaned one elbow against the door-jamb. "I'm not asking for your autograph. I'm asking for your company at dinner. What do you say?"

"I'd sooner eat sand."

"Hilary, your beer's getting warm."

"My name is not Hilary. It's Holly Hamilton, and I didn't agree to have dinner with you. I want you to go away. Now." She moved toward the screen door leading from the porch into the cottage.

"Holly Hamilton," he repeated. "Will it be Holly Hamilton tomorrow too? Or should I just call you the Glory Girl?"

"Go away!" She walked into the house, letting the inside door bang behind her.

Evan took a deep breath. He wasn't about to barge into her house, even if he owned it. Not yet, anyway. But, come hell or high water, they were going to talk.

"I said, 'should I just call you the Glory Girl?'"

Holly was out of the house and across the porch in two seconds. "*Shhhhh!* Do you want the whole Jersey shore to know I'm here?" she whispered, her hands flailing the air.

"Would that get you outside?" His tone softened. "Glory Girl, I need to explain a few things, and so do you. Would you have dinner with me?"

Holly rubbed the back of her wet leg with her toes while she mulled over his words. It was his property; he didn't have to go away. In fact, he could order her to leave at any time. Or make an announcement to the press that she was here. She sighed deeply. He sounded so sincere, so normal. She stared past him at the cloudless sky. The smell of charcoal starter and smoke were mingling with his after-shave. If she didn't watch herself, she'd be giving him a second chance. She nibbled the inside of her lip. At that moment her stomach rumbled noisily.

"I heard that," he teased.

"Annie's supposed to have delivered my groceries by now," she said when her stomach growled again. "I'll be out in a minute, and I'm only doing this because I'm starving."

A few minutes later Evan watched her, dressed again in caftan, hat, and dark glasses, walk across the patio and sit down on a lounger. He wiped the back of his hand across his forehead and sipped his beer. She looked as if she'd just fallen out of a piñata. Her arms were wound tightly around her waist and, crossing one leg over the other, she began tapping the patio incessantly with her foot.

He squinted toward a willow, taking note of its barely moving branches. "Warm enough?" he asked, gesturing toward her garb with his beer bottle. "Wind chill's got to be all of about eighty-five degrees." He bowed gallantly while she picked up a chunk of bread and bit off a piece. "But, if you'd like to move closer to the fire . . ."

"Just cut the comedy and keep your voice down," she said in an alarmed whisper as she motioned with the bread. Most of the houses on the populated sections of the barrier island had been built closely together, but this was not the case for the Jamieson property. Evan's fenced land was situated on a corner and bordered by two empty lots. Even so, someone could be walking by this very second.

Evan set his beer on the table, scratched his head, and pulled a chair closer to her. Straddling it, he sat down and spoke softly. "Holly, I just arrived in town this morning and headed right out for Dune Island Beach. I swear to you, the first time I saw that poster was after you saw it. What is going on?"

She made a disgusted sound with her tongue and shook her head. "Why are you still pretending you don't know?"

"Pretending I don't know what? That Sea and Sun Interiors hung a poster of you in my spare bedroom when they redecorated last month? That I just took a shower with a bar of soap wrapped in your picture? Look, I've been out of the country for the last few months, but I still appreciate an American beauty when I see one, whether her picture's hanging on my wall or she's lying on a beach or sitting next to me." He reached out and took her hand. "What I can't understand is why all of this subterfuge?"

His hand was still cool from holding the bottle of beer. Suddenly she found herself fighting the urge to press his palm to her cheek. She didn't see a spark of dishonesty in those big blue eyes of his, only concern. Then he squeezed her hand, and all the vinegar on the tip of her tongue turned to honey. "You really don't know, do you?"

He shook his head slowly. "I really don't."

"Evan, because of that poster, I've become the flavor of the week. I'm fair game for any weirdo who comes along, and believe me, there are plenty of them. In a bar on Sixty-second Street my poster's been turned into a dart board. I've even had a male reporter follow me into a public rest room." She watched his eyebrows lift in surprise. She uncrossed her legs and leaned forward. "It's true. And my parents called me last week to tell me about some church group in the Bible Belt insisting the poster be banned because it's warping their children's minds." She pulled off her sunglasses. "Their children's minds," she repeated. "Do you have any idea how humiliating this is?" She leaned in toward him. "I don't want to be in *People* magazine or on *Geraldo,* all I want is to be left alone to get on with the rest of my life."

Evan squeezed her hand. "Holly, humiliating isn't the word I'd use to describe the poster. I think it's absolutely gorgeous. It's sweet, it's sassy, it's romantic, it's innocent, it's—"

"Innocent, my butt!"

"That too." He tried hard not to smile as that gorgeous tush of hers appeared in his mind's eye once again.

Holly jumped to her feet. "Evan!"

"Calm down, calm down." He was still holding her hand, and she sank back at his tugging. The brazen blue of his eyes softened with self-reproach. "Forget about the adjectives. Tell me why you posed for it in the first place. I mean, if you felt so opposed to it, why did you do it?"

If his tone had communicated anything but honest interest, she would have screamed. The laugh lines around his eyes deepened with concern when she didn't answer immediately. Suddenly she wished she could tell him everything. For now at least, she would tell him what she could.

"Evan, that's just it. I wasn't posing for the poster. It was about two years ago during the shoot for the Morning Glory bath products line. I was getting ready for the shampoo shot. I stood up to position the shower nozzle, and Stu called my name. By the time I heard the shutter snapping, it was too late. Stu promised he'd destroy the negative. I trusted him."

"Stu? Can't you sue this Stu guy? Isn't this photographer bound by some release you signed to use the photos only for the product?"

Holly rubbed her forehead. "At the time, this 'Stu guy' was my husband. What started as a piece of fun has turned into a very lucrative business move for him. You see, before the divorce I was his chief source of income. He hated losing my face and body." Holly winced. That had to be the most conceited statement ever made. "I know that sounds pretty awful, but I'm not talking about his emotional pain when I left him. I'm talking about the business part of our marriage. He was angry and insisted that if I wanted the divorce, he wanted all legal claims to my Morning Glory contract. By then I wanted out of the marriage so badly that I ignored my lawyer's warnings and signed over my Morning Glory rights."

The lines forming between Evan's eyebrows were deep and numerous. He probably thought she was the biggest fool who ever drew a breath. What was she doing telling this man about one of the worst periods of her life? She'd known Evan Jamieson less than half a day. Blood pounded painfully in her temples.

Evan got up and handed her the beer he'd opened for her. He turned his back and made a business of stirring the coals in the barbecue. "You don't have to explain the end of a marriage, Holly. I've been there myself."

She found herself staring at the sunburn on the back of his neck, and then her gaze strayed to the tender reddened skin behind his ears. Her Sir Galahad of the parking lot knew hurt, too, and it went deeper than his sunburn. She hadn't missed the slightly bitter edge to his voice.

Evan adjusted the grill, then forked on two steaks. "Doesn't Morning Glory Soap object to any of this?"

"I wish. Stu airbrushed the prop on the poster so it doesn't match the soap company's morning glory. And, according to my lawyer, they couldn't be happier. Their sales have increased dramatically since the poster came out."

"Holly, I still don't understand why you're hiding. You're a model. You gave up a certain amount of privacy along the way. What's the big deal?" He turned back to her when she didn't answer. Her spine had stiffened, and her lips were trembling the tiniest bit.

"But I'm not a model anymore. I want all of that to be over."

Evan shrugged. "Then allow it to be over. Give the media and the fans what they want. Do a few interviews and, before you know it, they'll move on to someone else. You're adding fuel to your own fire by tantalizing them with your absence."

"You don't understand. Stuart took . . . something from me . . . and I want it back."

"What was it?" Evan asked quietly. "What did he take?"

"Maybe the opportunity to do something worthwhile with my life. There are certain plans I've . . ." She paused before blurting out angrily, "He's taken my dignity."

Evan considered her impassioned statement. He turned the steaks, searing them with a sizzling hiss. "Dignity, when you get right down to it, is a very subjective concept."

"Then you understand perfectly."

He rolled his eyes to the sky, then back to her. An initial embarrassment he could understand, but only she knew the depth of her "humiliation." He'd be damned if he understood it. He watched as her chin lifted a little higher, a little too high. Then it hit him like a crosswind. She wasn't telling him all of it. There was something she was leaving out. Something that made her eyes glisten and her chin almost quiver. Something that had to do with her ex-husband, Stuart Hamilton.

Instantly Evan's heart went out to her. Trust me, Holly, he wanted to say, but he didn't. After a divorce, allowing yourself to trust again was the scariest thing of all. He wouldn't cajole her into telling him either. He wouldn't tell her about the ugliness of his own divorce. That was positively the last thing she needed to hear and, besides, it was the last thing he wanted to talk about. In fact, he'd never talked about it with anyone.

"So, what about your plans?" he asked evenly.

Holly stood up, opened a carton, and began

spooning potato salad onto his plate. "To stay right here," she mumbled.

He wasn't asking her about her immediate plans. He was asking about the plans her ex had some-how messed up, about the opportunity to do some-thing "worthwhile." Had she deliberately skirted his question? He decided not to press. All in good time, he silently reminded himself. "Your plans are to stay right here? You mean, right here inside the fence, inside the cottage?" he said.

"You got it. By the way, I like my steak medium rare."

"You're joking?"

She gave him a queer look. "No, I really like my steak medium rare."

He set the barbecue fork on the table, then picked up his beer. "Holly, I mean about staying here inside the fence. That's no way to spend your vacation. You simply can't do that."

She shoved the spoon into the carton and set it back on the table. Just as she'd thought. Once he'd heard about the tacky incident, he would want her gone. And what she'd told him wasn't the half of it. Folding her arms across her middle, she turned to face him. "Vacation?!" she exploded. "This isn't a vacation, Evan. Can't you understand that this is a self-imposed exile, that I'm in hiding until the world turns enough to expose someone else's butt. Meanwhile, I want to remind you that I've paid my rent."

Her dander was up again; this woman was not about to succumb to a bout of weepiness, Evan noted happily. "Hiding? Is that what you were attempting on a public beach this afternoon while wearing an orange bathing suit cut up to the equator? Then covering it with that thingamajig?"

"Liz Claiborne does not design thingamajigs. Besides, I didn't bring attention to myself this afternoon rubbing suntan oil all over my chest!" They stood toe-to-toe, glaring at each other, when someone rapped on the gate.

Holly's immediate response was to grab Evan by the shoulders and slouch to the level of his chest. "Oh my God! They've found me," she whispered frantically.

"Ow! My sunburn."

Holly pulled her hands from his shoulders. "Sorry," she whispered, then turned and ran for her cottage.

That was the second time today she'd disappeared in a whirl of turquoise, Evan noted wryly. He set his beer beside the salad and went to the gate. "Yes?"

"Evan? Is that you?" The owner of the voice gave a quick laugh and, before he could answer, continued, "It's Annie. What are you doing here? Never mind. First just help me. I can't juggle a box of groceries and work the latch too."

Evan opened the gate, and his hands were immediately filled with a box of groceries.

Annie stepped inside. "I thought you were in Peru."

"I own the place, remember?"

Ignoring the question, she asked one of her own. "Where is she?"

"In the cottage. Didn't Tally tell you not to rent this month?"

The trim, five-foot brunette in jeans and a Bruce Springsteen T-shirt held her ground. A sly grin creased her face. "You complaining or thanking me?"

Evan heaved a sigh. Annie knew him too well, and he could no more bluster her today than he could during their childhood. Besides, she'd proved more than satisfactory as a rental agent and friend over the years. "Me? Complain? Where did complaining ever get me with you?"

"Nowhere, handsome. Your secretary's doing her job. She called a while back and said the big house was being redecorated and that you didn't want either house put on the rental market for the rest of the summer."

"But you went ahead and rented the cottage."

All traces of humor disappeared from Annie's expression. "Only the cottage. Evan, Holly's in a real mess right now. She's been my closest friend since junior high. Tell me you and I aren't going to part company over this."

"Of course not. But what's her story?" He motioned with his chin. "Her real story."

Annie looked past Evan toward the cottage. "Best friends keep secrets. You'll have to hear it from her, if and when she wants to tell you. Besides, if I told you what her ex-husband's done, you wouldn't believe it."

Evan studied the short brunette. "It's not just that poster, is it?"

"Of course not. Once Holly had a moment to cool down, even she admitted it was pretty cute."

Holly shot past both of them, slammed the gate, and latched it.

"Annie, I thought you said I'd be alone."

Annie looked back and forth at the both of them as if they were crazy. "Hi, Annie. Great to see you, Annie. You did a great job with the last tenants, old friend. Thanks for helping me out in a pinch, dear."

Holly exchanged a sideways glance with Evan before she spoke. "Guess I'm sounding ungrateful. I'm a little jumpy. Bad day at the beach."

Annie held up her hands. "Bad day at the beach? Nonsense. No one has a bad day at the beach. That's bad for tourism." Annie gave her a hug. "Deep breath. Relax. Has Mr. Electric-Blue Eyes here been threatening you with eviction or something?" Both women looked at Evan.

"Hey, don't look at me. I'm just the porter around here. Where do you want this stuff?"

"Put it in her house," Annie said. Evan started to walk away. "And put the perishables in her refrigerator."

"If it's not too much trouble, maybe somebody could turn the steaks," he called over his shoulder.

Holly hurried to the grill, snatched up the barbecue fork, and turned over the meat. "Lemon Aid's supposed to be sending me an address list and mailing labels. You will let me know as soon as they arrive, won't you?"

"As your mail collector, I do solemnly swear."

"Thanks. You know, at this stage in my life I thought I'd be doing a lot more for Lemon Aid than typing address labels. I'm not really complaining about the typing, but I miss working in the Manhattan office. You know—"

Annie wagged her finger. "I'll tell you what I know. You've rearranged your life to help Lemon Aid, to help kids. You'll never be satisfied just licking envelopes and typing address labels. That's why you've got to do something about Stu and his threat."

"He hasn't called you, has he?"

Annie shook her head.

"That's good. I'm sure he would have if he thought I was down here." Holly stared off into space for a moment, then nodded. "Yes, I think that's a good sign."

"Holly, no communication is not necessarily a good sign when it comes to that snake in the grass. You've got to talk to him sooner or later."

Holly waved off the direction Annie's conversation was taking. "I can't think about Stu right now. Annie, I didn't sign a lease on this place. I think I could be homeless really fast here. Is Evan going to kick me out?"

"I doubt it."

"But if he does, what are my chances of finding another place?"

Annie's eyebrows lifted and held. "Slim to none. Look, you'd have nothing to worry about if you'd move in with us until you've settled this mess. Hasn't this solitary confinement taught you anything?"

"To appreciate my prison fan mail more."

"Ah, Holly, Tony means it when he says he'd love to have you."

"Your husband is one in a million, but I can't. I'd spend all my time hiding in your bathroom. Your neighbors and family drop in like snowflakes in February." She forked the steaks onto the holding rack above the grill. "What I have to do is convince 'Mr. Electric-Blue Eyes,' as you call him, to let me stay."

"You never met him, did you? All the girls called

him that when he was a teenager. By the time you started coming down to the shore, he'd already gone off to a university out west. Then he married out there, and she never liked it back here. She said Martha's Vineyard was more her style. They're divorced now."

"Any kids?"

"None. I think he wanted them, but she never seemed interested." Annie rubbed her brow. "I can't remember her name. Let me think a minute."

So Evan Jamieson had wanted children and his ex didn't. How sadly familiar that situation was, she thought.

"I remember now. Her name was Cynthia, and when Peter was just a baby he had the good manners to wet all over her."

Holly didn't bother to stifle her burst of laughter, and Annie soon joined her. When they'd both stopped, Holly asked, "Did you ever date him?"

Annie shook her head. "Back then I was too young by about six years. But I use to bug the hell out of him and his brothers and friends. Some of them dated my older sisters. I'd follow them up on the boardwalk and pop up when they least wanted me."

"That she did," Evan affirmed as he rejoined them. "Those were the days, weren't they, Annie? Pizza from the Cape Shell Café, plunking down quarters at the arcades, and sharing it all with a pretty girl."

Annie gave him a thoughtful look. "Things haven't changed much. You ought to get yourself up there. Lucky Duck has a few new games I think you'd like to try." She walked backward to the gate and opened it. "Then you can bring Holly some french fries. Hey, I've got to run." The gate clicked shut.

Holly looked at Evan and narrowed her eyes. "What are you smiling about?"

"The boardwalk," he said, forking the steaks onto their plates. "I haven't been there in years."

"Oh. Neither have I." She wrapped her arms around her waist and shook her head wistfully. "The ocean breeze. The smells. The sounds. The people. Nothing compares to that boardwalk on a hot summer night."

"Nothing," he agreed. He pulled out her chair and motioned for her to sit down. "Holly, I think I understand why you've chosen to exile yourself in Cape Shell."

"You do?"

"It's because of Annie, because you trust her." Evan watched her mouth soften and her shoulders relax. He felt an almost smug satisfaction. She would eventually tell him the real problem behind her exile, and whatever that problem was, he was going to help her with it. He was good at solving problems, damn good, and he'd never had such a beautiful client before. Propping his elbow on the table, he rested his chin in his hand and waited.

"You're right. I have plenty of friends in and out of this country, but none that I trust like Annie. We've been through so much together. You know, we bought our first lipsticks together. I was her maid of honor, and she even . . ." Holly stopped. She wasn't about to tell Evan about Annie's warning not to marry Stuart. Holly reached for the bottle of steak sauce and shook it vigorously.

Evan had always believed in facing problems

head-on. Hiding away on the Jersey coast didn't seem right. Not for Holly Hamilton, at least. From the short time he'd spent with her, he'd already decided she was a gutsy woman. A woman who needed to be getting on with her life. "Holly, I don't know if this is going to work."

A piece of potato almost made it to Holly's mouth before she replaced it on her plate. He wanted her to leave and to take her half-told tawdry little problems with her. For the next minute the loudest sound was that of two impatient sea gulls perched on the gate's lampposts. As they screeched for food, their determined cries began to grate on Holly's nerves.

Evan continued to rest his chin in his hand. "Okay, what is it? What's got you so"—he fluttered his other hand—"so quiet all of a sudden?"

"Mmmm. Nothing," she replied in monotone. "This is so delicious. The steak's perfect. And you were very nice to ask me to dinner."

He smiled stiffly at her response. This strawberry-blond, green-eyed beauty was challenging his control in more ways than one. "If there's anything I can do to help you, if you need anything, all you have to do is ask."

She looked at him uncertainly. It appeared he wasn't kicking her out tonight. "Well, maybe there is something."

Evan folded his hands, rested them on the edge of the table, and leaned forward. Now he was getting somewhere. "Yes? Go ahead."

"Well. I don't know how to say this without sounding demanding."

He leaned forward a little more and nodded. "It's all right, Holly. Feel free to just speak your mind."

"That old air conditioner in my cottage conked out three days ago. I was wondering if you had an extra fan I could use."

Evan exhaled, closed his eyes, and slumped back against his chair. "A fan? You need a fan? That's it?"

"Yes."

"I'll get you a fan." He rubbed his forehead. It was obvious that she didn't trust him. Not yet, anyway. What he needed to do, he supposed, was to show her how. He'd simply have to open up to her. "I'll be right back," he explained as he left the table and went into his house. In a few minutes he returned to the patio.

"I thought you went to get the fan."

"Later. Holly, we need to talk some more."

Her jaws suddenly clamped shut on a mouthful of food as he placed her car keys beside her plate. Confusion clouded her eyes, and then she started chewing and swallowing at a rapid rate. When her mouth was empty, she swiped at her lips with a paper napkin and pushed up from the table.

"How long were you planning on keeping these?" she asked, snatching them from the table.

"Not too long."

She turned and headed for her cottage, managing to trip over the hose for the second time that evening.

Evan shot to his feet. "Hold on a minute. I'm not sorry I took them."

She whirled around. "Not sorry?! My mother *was* right, I never should have accepted a ride with a stranger."

"Holly."

He'd lowered his voice, and in doing so, tapped

into her spiraling emotions, scattering her fury like hot air. What was it about him that drove her nuts? And what was it about him that demanded sanity?

"Yes?"

He walked over to where she stood, picked up the hose, and tossed it toward the far side of the patio. "Keeping the keys wasn't so terrible, once you understand why I did it."

He slid his fingers under her chin. "Look at me. That's it." He smiled, and she found herself taking an extra breath. "It's true what I told you in the car. I saw you looking at me today on the beach. And I was looking back. I wanted to meet you, but before I could think of a nonmoronic way to do it, you'd left."

"Evan—"

He held up his other hand. "So I'm not sorry I kept the keys. Keeping them seemed like the only chance I had to spend time with you. I'm giving them back now because I want to begin this relationship in total honesty."

"Relationship? But Evan, you don't understand."

"Trust me, Holly, because sooner or later, I intend to understand everything."

"I can't—"

He leaned down. "Shhh. I'm going to kiss you."

"Ohh."

As his mouth closed over hers, a shiver of excitement swept through her. A part of her had been waiting for this kiss since he'd held her against the bedroom wall, and maybe even before then. Responding to his kiss was the easy part, controlling her response was not. As he drew her closer, enfolding her in his arms, she fought the urge to reach up and sink her fingers into his hair, to part her lips for his gently probing tongue, to moan from the want of sweet surrender.

Blood raced through his body at a pounding speed. He hadn't had such a lightning-quick reaction to a kiss since his teens. He broke the kiss slowly, pulling back finally when she opened her eyes. Maybe it was the sun and salt air that made him feel this way, he reasoned, looking at Holly's sunburned nose and soft smile. Or perhaps it was the memories this place evoked, he reasoned further, looking at her slightly parted lips. He looked her up and down and felt something catch in his stomach. The reason he felt this way wasn't because of a yesterday, it was because of Holly.

How quickly he'd caught on. Evan Jamieson, pooh-pooher of horoscopes, scoffer of biorhythms, skeptic of all "proven" miracles, was being struck by the proverbial thunderbolt. Kismet existed, born again in Holly's jade-green eyes. There was a hunger there he suspected would have shocked her if she could have seen it. There were clouds there, too, but no one could deny the glorious fact that Holly Hamilton needed him. As a friend, a confidant . . . and a lover. For now he'd have to convince her that he would be her friend. Soon, he'd be her confidant. Later, when it was right, he would be her lover. He knew in this moment that it was a fait accompli.

"You can trust me. Believe me. You can depend on me like you depend on Annie, only I'll be right across the patio. For the rest of the summer. And if I have to go to my North Jersey office, I'm just a phone call away."

A slow smile of relief lit her face. "You mean it? I can stay?"

It wasn't the response he'd hoped for or even the explanation he wanted to hear. It wasn't the cathartic rush of words he needed to hear, either, but it was a step in the right direction. Forward. "Yes, you can stay."

Three

Holly liked the decisive *bang* of her screen door as she crossed the wide patio heading toward the gate. A moonlit swim was exactly what she needed. During the day Cape Shell's beach was too crowded to attempt a swim, and because of yesterday's fiasco the less crowded Dune Island State Park was now off limits too. She closed her hand over the gate latch and sighed. Since she'd met Evan Jamieson, cabin fever had taken on a deeper meaning.

She lifted the latch, eased open the gate, and peered out. Not a soul around. The night was blessedly still outside the Jamieson property. Still, she had to be careful; night jogging and dog walking were popular pastimes in the family-oriented New Jersey resort town. Holly swallowed. An overzealous reporter was not an impossibility either. Across the road paralleling the beach and the boardwalk, the streetlights shimmered menacingly. Beyond those lights the deserted beach beckoned.

Thank goodness Evan was at his North Jersey office and not in his upstairs window looking out. What a comical sight she would have made as she hobbled, barefoot and wincing, across the pebble-strewn blacktop. Next time she decided on a midnight outing, she swore to herself, she'd remember to wear shoes.

Heading up the pedestrian ramp, she paused to look north. One mile away a canopy of colored lights glittered against the jet sky. Underneath, a few thousand people were enjoying the unique experience of a summer night on a livelier section of Cape Shell's boardwalk. With a slight wind out of the north, she started to imagine she could hear the arcade hawkers and smell the sausage and peppers grilling in the open air. Nameless emotions stirred, bringing back moments from her youth. Moments she'd started to recall at dinner last night with Evan.

Holly clutched the towel to her breast and thought of him with his sunburned ears and his questioning eyes. With his hair lifting and falling on his forehead in a warm breeze. She pressed the towel against her heart and shivered with the next memory: his mouth on hers.

Evan, who'd disturbed her in such an endearing manner. Evan, with his hard, muscled body begging to be touched. Evan, with his voice vibrating nerve endings she'd forgotten she possessed.

Weren't those visions of Evan the reason she'd decided on this midnight swim? She slipped her fingers through her hair and gave a little tug. She could not, she reminded herself, afford to indulge in any more thoughts like that. Thoughts might lead to actions, and actions to reactions. It was easy, so easy, to picture herself in Evan's arms. Turning toward the water, she hurried down the steps and out onto the sand. There was no denying their attraction for each other. Holly kicked hard into the sand. No denying, but no yielding to it, either. Once her unsavory secret was out, he would despise her. Those beautiful blue eyes would turn to steel once he knew the truth. Once everyone did.

Of all she'd been through this past year, she knew instinctively that Evan Jamieson's disapproval would be the one thing to finish her. So one way or another, she was going to stay away from Evan Jamieson.

Moonlight dappled the surface of the ocean invitingly. A bracing plunge and a rough swim would help her forget for awhile. She dropped her towel onto a twisted portion of weathered fence and made a run across the cool sand.

Finishing a second Creamsicle that night, Evan was heading upstairs for the third time. He was having a hard time falling asleep. The different bed, he told himself. Or maybe it was company business niggling at his mind. Louis Stoddard had insisted Evan was the only person he'd allow contract negotiations with, and so on the second day of his vacation Evan had gone to Stoddard's Manhattan office. The only thing pleasant about the two-hour return drive down the congested Garden State Parkway was that he was heading back to Holly. So he was disappointed when, on his arrival, her cottage was already dark.

For the umpteenth time he found himself glancing out the window on his second-floor landing. He tapped the pane with the clean wooden ice-cream stick. "Wake up," he muttered softly. "I've missed you, Glory Girl."

Bright and beautiful Holly with her secret. What was he letting himself in for? he wondered. Then the memories of her jade-green eyes flashing in anger when she'd seen the poster on his wall, sparkling with relief when he told her she could stay, and closing softly as he kissed her tripped across his mind. Holly with her endlessly long legs. Holly stumbling over the garden hose. Holly's skin beneath his fingers.

Evan chewed the little wooden stick. How had she taken possession of his mind and body in less than forty-eight hours? Evan Allen Jamieson, head of a multimillion-dollar company, a qualified pilot in four different aircraft, and select negotiator to Louis Stoddard, was bewitched, smitten, enchanted, and just plain thunderstruck with the Glory Girl. He was also thirty-four, divorced, and had not just fallen off the proverbial turnip truck when it came to women.

He rolled his eyes heavenward and pleaded. "A sign, just give me a sign. Something that—"

A noise out on the street interrupted his thoughts, bringing him back to the rational, reasoning person he was. Snapping the ice-cream stick in half, he reminded himself he was not entering puberty. Tomorrow he'd reevaluate Holly's situation. Yes, that was it. Examine the facts coolly, weigh the known against the unknown. Then get to work at uncovering the unknown.

Evan walked down the hall with a new resolve. Things had a way of working out. All he had to do was keep a cool head. And find out who was making all the racket in his front yard. He quickened his steps. Probably just a few teenagers harmlessly celebrating summer.

The shouting got louder.

"Jeese." Was he ever this loud at that age? Entering his bedroom, he strode across celery-colored carpet and pushed open the balcony doors. From his vantage point some fourteen feet above he could see three young men out on the sidewalk. He could also see Holly Hamilton pressing against his privacy fence as she crouched behind a shrub not five feet from the young men.

"Idiot!" one of the boys shouted to another.

"You lost her?" another shouted. "How in Alpha Chi's name could you lose her? I swear you'd lose your—"

Evan reached behind him and flicked on the spotlights. "Excuse me," Evan whispered loudly.

Three faces looked up toward the balcony, their eyes squinting in the spotlight's glare. Evan leaned over the balcony rail and stared down at them. "Could you keep it down? My wife just got the baby to sleep in there," he said, pointing over his shoulder.

Although she was well hidden in the shadows, Evan could see Holly's mouth open then close quickly. Now if she'd only trust him on this, he'd have her safe within the fence in half a minute.

"Sorry," one said. "It's just . . ."

Another picked up the line. "The Glory Girl. We

think we've spotted her, but bat brain here," he said, indicating one of his friends with a punch to his shoulder, "lost her."

Evan leaned over the railing and feigned lusty interest. "Really? The Glory Girl, the one with the, uh . . ." He traced the traditional feminine form with his hands as Holly glared up at him.

"Yes!" the threesome shouted from below.

Evan nodded, then rocked on his heels. "Well, I did see someone in a bathing suit rush by here a few minutes ago. She got into a, now let me see," he said slowly. "A van. That's it, a light-colored van."

"Which way was it headed?" asked the one rubbing his shoulder.

"Ah, forget it, dork," said another. "She could be anywhere by now." He looked up at Evan. "Thanks. Sorry if we woke your kid."

"No problem," Evan answered back in a stage whisper. He watched them walk to the corner and waited until they'd disappeared around it.

Leaning his elbows on the wrought-iron railing, Evan rested his chin in the cup of his hands and stared down at Holly. Still pressed against the wall, she'd sunk to her haunches and had dropped her forehead against her knees.

"Hello, down there."

Immediately she twisted her head up in his direction and mouthed the words, "Are they gone?"

"Yes."

She struggled to her feet as she brushed leaves and sand from her body. "You don't have to sound so smug."

"I don't, that's true," he said in a purely conversational tone. "Then again, you ought to have seen this from *my* viewpoint."

Holly sighed. "Well, you may as well double your smugness and get it over with. I forgot my gate key. Hey, aren't you supposed to be in North Jersey or Manhattan?"

"I'm back."

"I can see that!"

"Shhhh. You'll wake the baby. . . ."

Holly pushed her way free of the shrub and onto the sidewalk as she glared up at him again. "You don't have a baby up there."

She was wearing her orange swimsuit, and her hair, still wet from the ocean, clung to her shoulders in thick locks. Sand coated her legs like a dusting of light-brown sugar, and that suit, that suit that reached to the equator, stuck tightly to her body like plastic wrap. Evan sighed.

She stared up at Evan. He hadn't changed his stance; he continued smiling at her. "What are you staring at?" she demanded.

"You."

She wrapped her arms around her waist and, staring down at her toes, her legs, her body, asked indignantly, "What's so funny?"

"You are," he said. He pushed up from the rail.

Funny? He thought she was funny? She shifted her weight from one leg to the other. Should she be upset? she wondered. Or should she be delighted that she'd amused him and he cared enough to tell her so? Somehow she liked making him smile. On some unexplored feminine level it tickled her. She smiled back.

"Holly, why were you swimming alone out there

at this time of night? It's dark and dangerous as hell in that water."

He wasn't kidding; his tone was deadly serious now.

"I had to get out of there," she said, pointing over the fence. "I needed the exercise."

"You weren't frightened? Didn't you see that movie about the shark?"

"Evan, I'm a big girl. Right or wrong, I make my own decisions." She was practically shouting at him. If she didn't watch it, the boys would be back chasing her. Quietly she asked, "Could we talk about this inside the gate?"

"Good idea."

In less than a minute he was out of the house and releasing the gate latch. The gate sprang open, and Holly was through it like lightning. Instantly she backed against the fence, spread-eagle fashion.

"I thought I heard someone." She closed her mouth and forced herself to breath deeply through her nose.

"Do you ever do anything calmly?" Staring at her heaving chest, he realized he was feeling anything but calm himself. The thin material of her suit accentuated the swell of her breasts and the pebbly outline of her nipples. The tugging in his gut was starting again. Come to think of it, the tugging had begun the first few moments he'd seen her on the beach and had never completely stopped. And why should it stop? he asked himself. Had she any idea what her uneven breathing was doing to his?

She finally managed a whisper. "I can't remember."

Evan blinked. "Can't remember what?"

"The last time I had a calm moment." Her gaze traveled over his body. "Evan?" she whispered conspiratorially.

The tugging had taken on a wrenching quality. He reached out to trace her cheek with his fingertips and decided in that instant that he liked her best breathless. "What is it?"

The waistband of his pale-blue trunks rested dangerously low on his hips, exposing a vertical line of crisp hair below his navel. "Evan, you're in your underwear."

"I sleep in my underwear." Leaning closer, he inhaled deeply. She smelled of sea water and cherry candy. "What do you sleep in?"

She slept nude and had no intention of telling him. And even if she wanted to, how could she tell him anything with his lips skimming hers?

Evan stepped closer. The cool curves of her breasts pressed against his chest. Her lips were cool and sea salty on his tongue. He probed gently, and her lips parted. Groaning softly, she shifted against the intrusion of his touch. Slipping his hands over her hips, he pulled her closer. "Kiss me, Holly."

Holly pushed slowly off the fence and into his embrace. Evan's arms and the shadows of the night closed around her. Strong arms held her, protected her. No one could hurt her. Not while Evan held her so close and kissed her so deeply. She moaned softly from relief and from desire as she drank in the sensations. With his thighs pressed against hers and the heated flesh of his arms across her back, the rest of the world disappeared. His hard determination was melting her, making it impossible to think of anything but making love with him. But giving in to her own desire and his would complicate their lives. Making love would result in no good for either of them. No matter how badly she desired him, she couldn't do it. To him or to herself.

Here and now he wanted her. To hell with the world, he wanted her so badly it pained him. He slipped his fingers inside the straps of her suit and slid them down her arms.

"No," she whispered, pulling back. She made a business of adjusting the straps of her swimsuit. If she didn't watch it, she'd be trusting him with everything. "This is crazy. I can't."

Taking a step back, he rubbed his hand over his mouth. A slight tremor coursed through his body, and then he was in control again. "You're right. We're not a couple of teenagers." He took a huge breath and smiled at her. "We just feel like them. Come on, let me walk you back to your door where we'll shake hands good night."

"Like on a first date?"

He nodded.

Shaking his hand was safer than kissing him. Unsatisfying, but definitely safer. Evan's kisses were not meant for endings, they were meant for beginnings. She shivered at the delicious thought.

"Are you getting a chill?"

"A little. I dropped my towel when they started chasing me." She rubbed her arms.

"Sorry I don't have my letter sweater to wrap around you." They began a slow stroll across the patio. "I'll remember to bring it on our next date." He pointed back to the attic of the huge house. "My mother's got it packed away up there with—"

"Evan, we can't have a next date. You know I can't . . ."

"Playing hard to get, are we?"

She decided not to pursue the conversation, even if he was keeping it on a light note. When they arrived at the cottage she reached for the door handle. She was almost home free. Once inside she wouldn't be tempted to give in to the flood of feelings rushing through her. Once inside she wouldn't have to stare at her feet while trying to avoid staring at him. Once inside the temptation of Evan Jamieson would cease.

He reached out to take her hand.

"Holly?"

One more kiss, that's all, she promised herself. Reaching up, she wrapped her fingers around the nape of his neck and pulled his mouth to hers. This time she explored. This time her tongue did an erotic dance inside the warm cavern of his mouth. Quick and hungry and thorough. Then it was over, and she was inside her screen door and heading for her living room.

He clawed the screen. "Hey, I just wanted to shake your hand."

Holly stood stock-still as she listened to Evan whistling "As Time Goes By" while he made his way back across the patio. When he'd slid his door shut, she went into her tiny living room and sat down on the sofa. And laughed. Evan. Precious, sexy Evan. Teasing, intoxicating Evan. Evan. She laughed until the tears slid down her face. And then she began to cry.

Four

Dissolving into tears wasn't going to make her dilemma disappear. Talking to the perpetrator might. Holly swiped away the tears, then reached for her telephone receiver.

Four . . . five . . . six rings. Stuart's answering machine clicked on. Holly spoke evenly over the recorded greeting.

"Pick up the phone, Stu. I know you're there."

In a matter of seconds Stuart Hamilton picked up his phone and switched off his recorded greeting. He chuckled in a self-satisfied tone. "Well, what can I do for us?"

"It's been over three weeks since you told me about the negative for a second poster."

"And a profitable three weeks for some of us, Holly. Each passing day adds to the mystery surrounding the Glory Girl. Is she out of the country? Around the corner? Will we see more of her?" Stu laughed. "Got to hand it to you, you have a knack for baiting the public."

"I'm staying out of the limelight because my public life is over."

"Is it?"

Holly froze. Had Stu figured out her plan? Becoming the national spokesperson for Lemon Aid would keep her in the public spotlight. Of course, all of it hinged on being named to the board of directors, and that wouldn't be decided until autumn. She still had time to deal with Stu's threat.

"If my absence happens to sell a few more posters, making you a little richer, it isn't important to me, Stu."

"But I know what is important to you, and you can have it if you'll come back to work."

"Stu, why can't you understand that I'm not—"

He cut in quickly. "Did you listen to Dennis Cracci's six o'clock entertainment report tonight? I would have called you, but all you've given me is your lawyer's number. Anyway, he's offering two round-trip tickets to Montego Bay for anyone finding the Glory Girl. That reporter's done more for poster sales than I ever thought possible."

"We need to talk about the second negative."

"What's there to talk about? I want you back to work for me." His voice had dropped, and his words came menacingly fast. "I mean it, Holly. Enough of your hide-and-seek."

"Be reasonable. You took advantage of me. You took both photos and kept them without my permission. You're not being fair."

"Holly, love, you signed over all rights from that photo shoot. Those two photos and their negatives belong to me. Actually, the first kind of belongs to the public now. If you're interested in owning the second one, all you have to do is come back to work."

She was dealing with a pigheaded jackass. The shock of it was, she'd once been married to him. "I don't even know what this second photo looks like."

"Holly, if you put off the inevitable much longer, soon everyone will know exactly what it looks like."

He wasn't letting up. He was just as determined to manipulate her life to his benefit as he ever was. Holly paced in front of the sofa as anger inside her began to build.

"One more chance, that's all I'm asking, Holly. I've accepted that we'll never be man and wife again, but we were a damn good business team. Your face and figure and my Hasselblad. What do you say, honey? Will you come back to work?"

"No."

"You can do all the volunteer work you want. Lemon Aid can have their precious envelope stuffer."

"No."

"Then you have until September before the Glory Girl Two is unveiled. And it's everything you've imagined it to be."

"*September*? Stuart, please don't do this. You don't need me. You're bound to find a new face soon. There are plenty of willing models. Give them a chance. That's what the ad agencies want. New faces. You can do it, Stu."

"Of course I can do it," he snapped. "I don't need you to tell me that."

"Look, I'm going forward, Stuart, not backward. This sword you have dangling over my head, this second picture I've never even seen, is a rotten thing to do to me. It's unfair. What have I done to hurt you so much?"

"*Hurt* me? Is that what you think you've done? It's business, Holly." He laughed triumphantly. "Business. It's always been business. Call me when you come to your senses. But I'm not waiting forever." He hung up.

Holly replaced the receiver and walked numbly out onto her screened porch. She lit the candle jars, and in their pulsating glow closed her fingers around the arm of the swing and sat down. Flexing her knees, she pushed the swing into motion as Stu's words echoed in her ears.

"It's always been business," he'd said.

Why hadn't she seen it from the beginning? How had she ever stayed married to him for over three years? She dropped her head on the back of the swing and thought back to the very beginning.

Straight out of college she'd gone to New York, looking for a job in journalism. Stu had seen her in a restaurant dining with friends and approached her with an offer that had been lifted out of a movie script.

"I want to photograph you for a Mariposa perfume ad. Your look is perfect for it."

Holly thought his "I'm gonna make you a star" line was hilarious. She was ready to laugh off the offer from the insistent blond, bearded man, but her girlfriends assured her it would be an adventure she'd never forget. They even volunteered to accompany her to his studio. With her money running out and no journalism job in sight, Holly said yes.

No doubt about it, Stu knew his work. The perfume ad led to a coffee ad, and that led to a national fast-food commercial. One booking followed another, and soon her personal life and work life began blending with Stu's. He talked about commitment, about growing together, about a happy, successful life where they could both find fulfillment. How wonderfully like her parents' marriage he'd made their future sound. Fulfillment to her had meant eventual marriage and children. For all Stu's bravura, she'd wanted to believe he had a softer emotional side that would lend itself well to raising a family. His first marriage didn't work out because he and his wife had nothing in common, but he and Holly, he explained, were so much alike. His casual proposal, she later explained to Annie, was all in keeping with his sense of humor.

"Our life would be a lot easier if we got married. What do you say?"

During a short honeymoon involving two photo shoots in the Caribbean, her first doubts started emerging. Work was his only world. Stu had wedded her in a marriage of convenience. His convenience. His favorite model had become his wife.

After she'd signed as top model with a cosmetic company, the money began pouring in. Financially secure now, she suggested they work less and enjoy life more. Stu laughed. After months of trying in subtle ways to change the parameters of their marriage, Holly decided to put her foot down.

"We're going to start living a normal life, Stu, or I'm leaving."

"What do you want? A plant? A bird? A house in the Hamptons? What? Name it."

"A baby."

"And ruin that figure? Hey, parenthood isn't what it's cracked up to be. I ought to know, I'm paying child support for two."

"Money. Is that all you ever think about? Does everything and everyone have to be measured in dollars?"

He waited a long time to answer. "There won't be any children. I had a vasectomy after my second kid."

She couldn't have felt more stunned if he'd slapped her. "You—you never said—"

He shrugged. "I'm saying it now. Get used to it."

That afternoon she saw a lawyer and started divorce proceedings. She hadn't failed at her marriage; she'd never really had one to fail at.

Holly pushed the swing again, almost blissful in the emotionless void surrounding her. Stuart had probably never loved her. She examined the effect that statement had on her as she repeated it again and again. Nothing. No twinge in the heart, no tearing in the eyes. As a matter of fact, she began to feel a tremendous sense of well-being.

Holly reached up and stretched luxuriously. That last fragment of guilt over initiating her divorce vanished along with some unnameable obligation. She looked across the patio at Evan's house and smiled. A few minutes later she was back in the cottage and in bed. She lay there feasting on the feelings of relief and wishing she had someone to share them with. Evan Jamicson came to mind again. But his shining image dimmed quickly with the next logical thought. Holly punched her pillow in disgust. One explanation would lead to another, and then he would know about the second negative. And how would he react when she told him she had no idea how revealing the second poster was? That Stu had shot her a second time as she was emerging from the flower prop . . . as she was turning toward him . . . naked. The second poster, if printed, might have to be sold in a plain brown wrapper. As a children's charity, Lemon Aid wouldn't want her on its board and definitely not as its spokesperson. Whom was she kidding? If that second poster came out, Lemon Aid wouldn't let her lick a stamp. Holly covered her head with her pillow. Her problems were far from over.

The next morning the telephone rang at six-thirty. Even in her groggy state she remembered not to speak in case Stu was the caller.

"It's okay, Holly. It's me, Annie. I need a favor."

Holly yawned and pulled the receiver under the pillow along with her head. "Anything you want, friend."

"I'm taking you at your word. My sitter's sick, and Tony and I are up to our elbows in buttered rolls and morning coffee. Could you watch the kids today?"

Three-year-old Paula and five-year-old Peter were bundles of energy. If only for the day, the twosome would take her mind off her problems. "I'd love to. Bring them over."

Two hours later Holly sat on a bench in the tiny garden behind the cottage, French braiding Paula's hair. Peter was telling them both a story about a dinosaur living under his bed.

"Is he scary?" asked Holly.

"No," piped in Paula. "He not a scary 'saur."

"Right," said Peter. "But he's real gross. He eats my spinach and drinks my dad's beer. When he gets all filled up, he burps. Yuck—it's the grossest smell you ever smelled."

Paula clapped her hands. "Yuck," she added.

"And," continued Peter, "when Uncle Evan came over last night, he fed him my shoes. We can't find them anywhere. That's why I get to wear my cowboy boots." He stomped the bricks beneath him in case Holly hadn't noticed the fancy red boots.

Holly stopped braiding. "Uncle Evan came to your house last night?"

"Yep. It was real late, but I was awake. He asked my mom all about you."

Holly felt her cheeks flame. Calm down, she told herself. If there was one person she could trust, it was Annie. If Annie had told Evan about the second negative and Stu's threat to print it, she would have mentioned it this morning when she'd dropped off the kids.

"Don't you want to know what Uncle Evan asked my mom?" Peter demanded.

"Yes," demanded a deeper, more masculine voice from behind the bench. "Don't you want to know what I asked his mom?"

Prickles spread across Holly's shoulders, but for the moment she said nothing. She tied off Paula's braid and kissed her. Without standing up, she turned to face Evan.

"Do I?" Their gazes met and locked.

"I can tell you," announced Peter. "I was there and I can—"

Holly cut in on the little boy's earnest offer. "It's not right to tattle, Peter. Take your sister's hand

and show her the tomato plants over there. You can each pick one tomato."

Peter made a dissatisfied noise in his throat, but took Paula's hand and led her away.

Holly's gaze resettled on Evan. He was freshly shaved, his hair still bore teeth marks from his comb, and, even considering how mad at him she was right now, he still looked wonderful. If she had any doubt about just how wonderful, that swirling shiver in the pit of her stomach confirmed it. How utterly delicious he looked this morning.

Evan strained to look around Holly. "Tomatoes? Who planted tomatoes back here?"

"Your last tenants. According to Annie, they left to join a commune in West Virginia right after they put them in."

"Really?" He started for the plants.

Standing quickly, Holly's hand shot out and grabbed his wrist, stilling him in his tracks. "Just a minute, Mr. Landlord. About my privacy and your lack of respect for it . . ."

He looked her up and down. She'd tied up her hair in a casual ponytail, and already springs and coils of golden red were forming around her face. The lemon-colored ruffles on her halter dress undulated in the breeze. He wondered if morning glories came in yellow, but by the straight line her lips made thought it best not to ask her. Instead, he touched the tip of her nose, which was thickly coated in pink zinc ointment.

"You look like you had a fight with a cupcake and the cupcake won."

She dropped his wrist and stepped back. "Speaking of noses, why can't you keep yours out of my business?"

"I already told you. Sooner or later I'm going to find out what's really keeping the Glory Girl inside my fence. Besides, you practically attacked me at your door last night, and my virtue is not to be taken lightly. I came for an apology."

She shook her finger at him while trying her darndest not to laugh. "You . . . ." she began. She laughed softly, shaking her head. "What am I going to do with you?"

Evan pulled her around the corner of the cottage, effectively cutting off the children's views. "For a start," he said, kissing the side of her neck, "you can begin trusting me."

For a long moment Holly stared into his eyes. They were absolutely the most beautiful shade of blue she'd ever seen. "Evan, there's so much you don't know."

"Hey, Holly, can I eat this?"

Both Holly and Evan turned to look at Peter. He'd come around the corner of the house clutching the biggest tomato Holly had ever seen. Holly's eyes rolled heavenward. Saved by a tomato. Thank you, God. "Great idea, Peter. Want to save it for lunch?"

"No, I want it now. On a hard roll. With mayonnaise. And a pickle. And I want Uncle Evan to have half of it."

Holly tilted her chin toward Evan. "Well, Uncle Evan?"

Evan nodded. "Fine with me, pardner, but what about your sister?"

Paula appeared from behind her brother with a cherry tomato in her hand.

"Dis a baby tomato," she announced before dropping it on Evan's bare foot. Her tiny hands came up quickly to cover her mouth. "Uh-oh. I broke it."

The bright-red fruit had splattered across Evan's toes. He wriggled them. "Indeed you have broken it. Hmmm. Well, we'll just have to let you pick another. Can you show me which plant you found that baby tomato on?" He swooped the little girl into his arms and walked toward the plants.

Holly watched as Evan covered the little girl's neck with dozens of wet, noisy kisses and listened as Paula shrieked with laughter. How perfectly joyous the scene was, the tall, broad-shouldered man playing with the child. For some unnameable reason Holly felt tears well up behind her eyes.

Peter patted Holly's leg. "Uncle Evan didn't kiss you like that, Holly. Do you want him to?"

"What? Oh. You saw Uncle Evan kiss me, did you?"

"Yeah. He kissed you right there," said Peter, pointing to the side of his neck.

Two hours had flown by, and Holly found herself tied to a tree in a shady corner of Evan's garden.

Peter patted the end of the rope in his hand. "She's my hostage now. How much money should I ask for her, Uncle Evan?"

Nearby, Evan sat on the grass with Paula in his lap. "How much do you think she's worth, cowboy?"

Peter pondered the question. "Well, I like her a lot. She took me to the big show at Radio City last Christmas. The one with camels and the soldiers that fall down. She's worth a lot. About a zillion dollars."

"Well, I have some change up on my dresser. Would you take eighty cents?"

Without a second's hesitation Peter agreed, and Evan sent him for the money.

Evan handed little Paula a plastic cup and pointed her in the direction of a trickling hose. He got to his feet and walked over to Holly. "My, my, what a pretty package. All tied up right here under my apple tree." He reached to stroke her jaw with his knuckles.

Holly pulled up her chin, but not so much as to break the tantalizing connection with his fingers. "Evan, don't you dare do anything in front of Paula that I will make you regret."

They both glanced at the little girl filling and refilling the plastic cup.

"But you heard her big brother," he said as he reached up and removed the tie holding her ponytail. "Give her a hose to play with, and you could ride a horse through here and she wouldn't know it." He leaned over and kissed her ear. Then he kissed her neck. Twice. Slowly. "I love the way your hair smells," he murmured.

"Evan," Holly whispered. "Please don't do that."

"How about if I do this?" He kissed her on the mouth. Softly.

She drew in a deep breath as sensations flowed through her body at an alarming speed. "I—I don't think that's such a good idea either."

"Oh, but I think it's a wonderful idea. In fact"—he paused to kiss her again—"I think you like it too."

Holly swallowed. It was hard to think while he

stroked the sides of her face with his thumbs.
"You're taking advantage of me. You shouldn't—"
She stopped talking as his lips brushed hers again.
"You . . . you . . ." He ran his tongue along her
bottom lip, prompting her to open it. With a slight
whimper she did. And then he took control of
her mouth and mind, filling them both with unquenched desire. Exploring the soft sweetness
there, his tongue deftly tangled with hers. Only
the slight pressure of the ropes held her back from
a full embrace. Suddenly she remembered that
Peter would be back at any moment. "Evan, we've
got to stop."

Evan did stop. He drew back his head, and for a
moment that seem to last for hours stared solemnly into her eyes. Then he slowly began to
smile. At first the corners of his mouth lifted, then
the laugh lines around his eyes increased and
deepened. A self-assured excitement sparkled in
his eyes. "We've got to begin. We both know that.
Don't we, Holly?"

It was more of a statement than a question, and
she knew it. Moreover, it was the truth. "Evan—"

Whatever she was about to say became lost in
the ensuing events. All at once Peter appeared
next to the tree, and Evan's pager sounded. "Holly,
Uncle Evan's got your picture upstairs. The one
that Stu the pooh took. The one without your
clothes. Did you know that, Holly?"

Holly cleared her throat. "Yes, Peter, I did know
that. And now that you have your ransom, you'll
have to untie me so we can play something else."

"Sure." Peter shoved the coins in his pocket and
began untying Holly. "Can I play with the hose
now? Paula's done with it."

Paula tugged on his pant leg, and Evan picked her up.

Holly gave Evan a knowing look. "Seems like you've got yourself a girlfriend."

"I want Bunny," whispered Paula, rubbing her eyes.

"Bunny's her rabbit," Holly explained. "He's in my cottage. Why don't you take her over there and put her in my bed? You can answer your pager from my phone. Meanwhile, I'll get Peter set up with the hose.

Ten minutes later Holly tiptoed through her living room and peeked around the doorway into her bedroom. Evan was just tucking in Paula and her beloved Bunny. He'd already turned on the window fan and lowered the shades. In the subdued light Holly watched as he kissed the little girl's forehead.

"Bunny too," Paula entreated.

"Bunny too," he replied before kissing the one-eared lavender rabbit. "Sleep tight, little one," he whispered.

Holly watched as he straightened up. He slid his hands into his pockets and gazed at the child for a few more seconds. Then he sighed so loudly; Paula turned in her sleep. He began backing out of the room, then seemed to change his mind and walked over to an electrical outlet. He knelt down to inspect it.

Holly shrugged off his spur-of-the-moment inspection and went out on the porch to wait for him. It shouldn't surprise her that he was inspecting an outlet; after all, he was the landlord.

When Evan walked out onto the porch, he had one question. "What happened to you?"

"Oh. Peter got me with the hose." She patted the sides of her face and looked down at her ruffle-tiered sundress. "Mostly he got me in the front."

"And you weren't wearing a T-shirt."

"How clever of you to notice." She pointed to the chair across from her.

Evan sank into the deep cushions of the old wicker armchair facing the swing. He waited until she'd repositioned herself on the porch swing, then lifted his feet beside her.

"That was one of my clients paging me," he said. "President of Stoddard, Inc. Owns about twelve different companies, but still likes to lease his jets from us."

"Is there a problem?"

"Could be. So far we've been able to satisfy his whims. For example, he insists all of his pilots must have twenty-five years experience, have gray or white hair, and not be allergic to dog hair." Evan flexed his knees, pushing the swing into motion.

"Dog hair," she repeated flatly.

"Mr. Stoddard sometimes travels with a shedding dog, which ought to be totally bald by now. The fact is, he's a friendly, fluffy, four-legged dust mop that howls during takeoffs and landings."

A young girl's giggle bubbled up in her throat, thoroughly delighting him. "I love it! You make your work sound like a glitzy sitcom. What's the problem?"

"We're renegotiating his contract. My sources have it that he's looking around at other jet-leasing firms. This isn't out of the ordinary, but it's something I have to keep on top of. Along with the fact that he's extremely image conscious. He's so conservative, he's almost stodgy."

She absently stroked the top of his foot. "I'm beginning to get the picture. What's going to happen if he finds a better deal?"

He shrugged, as if suddenly unconcerned with the matter.

She persisted. "But what's the worst thing that can happen?"

"I'd probably have to drop six pilots."

Her fingers tightened around his foot, and she jerked it. "*Six pilots?* You mean, at whim this man can cause six people to lose their jobs? That's so unfair!" She shoved his foot to the floor. "Evan, no one should have that much power over other people's lives. What are you going to do about it?"

Evan gave her a lazy smile. "Yours truly's going to do what he does best. I'll figure out a solution to keep everyone happy."

"Oh, you can do that?" she said, relaxing back against the swing once again. Her eyes lost their focus as she mulled something over. He watched her, waiting. Waiting.

One blink and she was back, away from that place she wouldn't share with him. He rested both elbows on the arms of the chair and studied her. "You have a strong sense of what's fair and what's not. Where does that come from?"

"Life's little experiences, but let's not get into that," she said lightly. She stretched her legs out along the length of the swing. "On to more important questions," she said, waving her arm with a flourish. "What are all those Creamsicles doing in your freezer, and why were you inspecting the electrical outlets in my bedroom?"

Their conversation was progressing pleasantly. Using her willingness to be touched and her laughter as a gauge, he decided she was definitely warming to him, beginning to let down her defenses, he decided. He didn't want her bolting now. He could wait a while longer to hear what kept her in the cottage.

He stood up and, looming over her, lifted a damp ruffle from the front of her dress. "Creamsicles and outlets are both very personal topics," he said, as he played with the shallow hem on her ruffle. "I'm going to ignore the first topic, at least until we know each other better. Much better. And as for the second, if you invite me over for dinner, I'll let you drag that explanation out of me after some slow torture. What do you say?"

He continued toying with the fabric, slowly rubbing it between his fingers. Touching her, yet not touching her. Close, but not close enough. A game of innocent teasing, that's all it was, she assured herself. She caught the gleam in his eye. A shivery sensation began in the pit of her stomach and surged upward until it became a smile.

"I'm not going anywhere. Why not? I'll call in an order to Annie, and when she picks up the kids she can drop the stuff off. Six o'clock sound okay?"

He reached behind her head and lowered his face closer to hers. "Six o'clock is a long way off," he whispered.

Six o'clock *was* a long way off, but by then she'd figure out a way to outmaneuver his romantic choreographies. His breath was warm on her lips. This was going to be the absolute last time she'd let him get this close. . . . Closer.

"Hey! You aren't going to let him kiss you again, are you, Holly?"

Holly and Evan turned toward the patio. Peter was slinging the hose over his head, using it as a lasso and getting himself soaked in the process. "Here come wet kisses, Holly," Peter shouted. A shriek of laughter cut through the screened porch, along with a well-aimed stream of water.

Five

Holly held a corkscrew in one hand, an unopened bottle of wine in the other, and the telephone receiver between her shoulder and ear. She leaned against the kitchen counter and squinted with confusion. "Evan, where are you? You sound so far away."

"Heading north on the parkway. I'm using my car phone. My pager beeped when I was dropping off the kids. Looks like I'm a no-show for our dinner tonight."

She placed the bottle and corkscrew on the counter, then took hold of the receiver with both hands. "Problems with that client?"

"And a few other things. I'm really sorry about this, Holly. I was looking forward to our evening together."

Holly slid onto the kitchen stool. "So was I," she confessed. "But we can have dinner tomorrow night."

"I'm not sure how long I'll have to be gone. I'll be

staying at my Manhattan apartment but working at the Teterboro office over here in New Jersey during the day. Annie has the phone numbers. Are you going to be okay?"

Everything she'd ever been taught about good posture fled her mind as she slouched over the counter and closed her eyes. He wasn't coming tonight. He wasn't coming tomorrow night. He wasn't sure when he was coming.

"Holly? Holly, are you there?"

She pushed up on one elbow and thanked her lucky stars he didn't have one of those videophones. It was, after all, just one dinner they'd planned on sharing, not the rest of the summer. Trying to keep her reply matter-of-fact in tone as well as in substance, she answered, "Yes, I'm here. I dropped the phone. And of course I'll be okay. I've been okay down here for almost a month now, remember?"

"I'll be back as soon as I can."

"Evan, I'm not your problem, and I don't want you to think of me as one. I'll be fine. Annie's here in town, and I do have things to do."

When she replaced the receiver depression settled over Holly like the unwelcome heat wave blanketing the shore. She was coming to realize she was not only getting used to having Evan around, she was also beginning to depend on him. And that really had to stop. So this separation was a good thing after all. She stood up and attempted to deliver a self-satisfied grin for the mirror. The reflection in the seashell-framed mirror wasn't very convincing.

"More fan mail, I think," said Annie, dumping the armload in Holly's lap the following day. "The kids got hold of it and destroyed the carton your lawyer sent it in."

Holly unceremoniously pushed the pile to the floor of the porch. "You know, you could have told me Evan had been to see you night before last, that he'd asked about me," she chided her friend.

Annie rolled her tongue inside her cheek. "I also could have told you we're ordering extra provolone and beer sausage for the Fiesta Fantasy Night crowd next week."

"This is different, Annie."

"I'm glad you're coming to realize that. You're already missing him, aren't you?"

Surprised and flustered, Holly broke their eye contact. "Well, a little. He's become a kind of friend and—"

"Holly, this is great! I should have gotten you two together years ago. Of course, he was married to Cynthia, and you—"

Holly moved to her feet. "Now wait a minute. Just what are you getting at? He's my landlord. A rather charming one with a great sense of humor. But just my landlord, all the same."

"Yeah. Right. Kiss, kiss."

Holly winced as she recalled yesterday morning in the tomato garden and how Annie's five-year-old had witnessed their kiss. It hadn't taken Evan's little "pardner" long to relate the big event to his mother. Folding her arms across her midriff, Holly turned away from her friend. "I don't know how that happened, and I certainly didn't mean for Peter to see it."

Annie laughed a short, delighted laugh. "Let me explain how it happened. First you put two good-looking members of the opposite sex together. Two pretty damn nice and pretty damn lonely people who deserve a second chance at happiness. If God wills it. . . ."

Whirling around, Holly threw up her hands. "Oh, Annie, don't bring God into this."

"And why not? Would you prefer the devil?"

"Annie, it was only a kiss."

"Was it?"

"Look, once Evan's vacation's over, he'll go back to work. I'll be nothing more than a memory. A project that occupied the mind of an intelligent, energetic, funny—"

"Handsome, sexy," Annie cut in.

"Will you stop it?"

"Can you?" Annie replied quietly as she turned to leave.

"Of course I can!" Holly shouted after her friend.

The gate clicked behind Annie. With a huffy sigh Holly bent to scoop up her mail. There was plenty to do today. She had lots of phone calls to make, so keeping Evan Jamieson out of her thoughts shouldn't be too difficult. She flipped through the envelopes, pulled the ones concerning Lemon Aid, and tossed the rest onto the wicker armchair. The same chair Evan had occupied yesterday.

Holly growled. He was present even when he wasn't! This was ridiculous. She hadn't planned on missing him. She rubbed her temples as more memories trickled into her consciousness. Memories of his fingertips fondling the ruffles of her dress, of his warm breath against her neck, of his hot mouth about to relish hers. Holly stood up, staring at the chair. It was going to be a long week.

She had to stop acting like a love-struck puppy mooning over her master's empty shoes. Looking at a newsletter from Lemon Aid, she decided to call the organization's headquarters. Ever since last month when she'd had to give up going into the Manhattan office, Dave had been her lifeline to the group. She'd be ever grateful for that, because their chatty newsletter wasn't very newsy when it came to office politics and the inner workings of Lemon Aid. With the board election coming up, she needed to keep informed.

"Hi, Dave. It's Holly."

"Hey, we miss our most productive volunteer up here. Where've you been lately?"

"I've had some personal things I've been trying to get out of the way. Believe me, as soon as they're taken care of I'll be back in my little cubbyhole."

Dave's tone changed from lighthearted to serious. "I hope that's soon. The rumor mill has it that the board is considering a few other names for the empty chair. For instance, Willoughby has a brother-in-law who wants it. I'd hate to see him get it, Holly, because he only wants it to see his name on the letterhead. Nobody cares about Lemon Aid as much as you."

"Thanks. What about the Glory Girl poster? How much damage has been done by that?"

"I thought an innocent peek at your tush was harmless entertainment, myself. Unfortunately, Willoughby doesn't agree. He's using it against you to push his brother-in-law onto the board. You should be up here reminding everyone what an asset you are to this place."

Going into the Lemon Aid office was next to impossible. She'd tried it after the poster came out, and the press practically opened the door for her. "Dave, I can't come in right now, but I'm doing some fund-raising on my own. I'll send in copies of the letters, and maybe if they fall into the right hands . . ."

"You know I'll make sure everyone gets copies, but Holly, keep in mind it isn't the same as being here. I think your best shot at the board is through replacing the memory of that poster with nine-to-five work right here."

Early the next evening Holly addressed the envelopes for eight fund-raising letters she'd worked on that day. She dutifully slipped copies inside a manila envelope addressed to Lemon Aid. She'd met plenty of wealthy people during her years of modeling, and many of those she knew to be kindhearted and giving. Those she'd chosen to write to would hopefully give generously to the children's organization. She licked the stamps, patted them into place, then stared at the thick pile. If Evan were here, she would have asked his advice because—Evan, Evan, Evan! He wasn't here, and he had no reason to advise her on anything to do with the organization.

But there was no denying his genuine affection for children. The vision of him playing with Peter and Paula came to mind. Holly laid her hand on the pile of envelopes, then pushed back her chair.

If he wouldn't leave her mind, she would. Holly repositioned the fans, poured a glass of iced tea, and turned on the TV. She settled back in a cushioned papasan and gulped her tea while she waited impatiently for the alpha waves to take her away.

An all-too-familiar voice filled the room. "Dennis Cracci here, giving you the latest update on our Glory Girl. Three reported sightings this week."

Holly sat bolt upright. Sightings? What did he think she was? A UFO?

"Our first report comes from Port Townsend, Washington, where twenty Boy Scouts insist they've seen our Glory Girl hiking in the Olympic National Park. In the beautiful wilderness area known as Hurricane Ridge, Holly Hamilton was spotted just two days ago. Alone."

Video taken during a drizzling rain showed Boy Scouts in ponchos pointing toward a neighboring mountain. A boy in rain-splattered glasses kept shaking his head.

"The next report comes to you from Cape Shell, New Jersey, where several vacationing college students, spending the summer there, are ready to bet their next year's tuition that Holly Hamilton is in town. We go live to Cape Shell's boardwalk with our own Bobbie Keith. Bobbie, what do you have for us?"

"Hi, Dennis. I'm live here on the boardwalk in Cape Shell with a group of young men anxious to talk about who they've seen here recently."

Holly slammed her glass on the coffee table and dropped forward out of the papasan and onto her hands and knees. "No, no, no," she begged, creeping closer to the set. Her plea was instantly answered. The three students who'd chased her from the beach a few nights ago exploded onto the TV screen with all their normal gusto.

"She's here, I swear it." The shirtless speaker in the colorful Jams emphasized his remarks by raising two fists into the air.

The pretty young female reporter adjusted her earpiece and continued, "When and where exactly did you see the Glory Girl?"

All three students spoke at once, and all three were giving different answers. "Dork," someone shouted. A disembodied arm intruded from out of the camera range, knocking the loudest speaker's baseball hat askew.

Holly blinked at the screen. Someone had evidently shoved into the cameraman, and the screen was now filled with sea gulls feasting on popcorn spilled across the boardwalk.

The picture bounced back to a midtown Manhattan studio. "We've lost our picture," Dennis Cracci reported redundantly.

Dennis adjusted his tie, shot a few nervous glances toward his monitor, and looked off camera for help. "Yes, yes," he mumbled. "Well, we're going now to Newport News, Virginia, where Madam Michiko is waiting to speak. Can you tell us where she is and if the rumor of a second poster is true? Go ahead, Madam Michiko."

Holly couldn't believe it. Dennis Cracci was sliding right by the Cape Shell report in favor of a bizarre psychic in a blond wig. While rubbing a crystal ball the size of a basketball she babbled in an unintelligible language. What a desperate man Cracci was turning into.

Well, at least the Cape Shell report appeared to be as ridiculous as the other two reports. No one in his or her right mind would take it seriously. She picked up the remote control and zapped Cracci and his cronies out of her living room. All the same, a certain unease made her look around the room. She climbed to her feet, walked over to the door, and looked outside. What she was looking for exactly she couldn't say. She stared at the gate and listened. The crickets hadn't changed their cadence. Everything looked the same. She leaned her head against the door and closed her eyes. How much more could she take? And how much longer could she take it?

The telephone rang. Holly caught her breath from the sudden sound, then calmly reached over and picked up the receiver. She waited.

"Holly? It's Evan."

A rush of air escaped her lips. "Evan, it's so good to hear your voice." Why was she saying *that*? Even if it was true, she didn't have to admit it. Desperation was the last thing she wanted him to hear in her voice.

"Good to hear yours too. For a moment I thought you'd taken off for the rain forest on the Olympic peninsula."

He'd seen the report too. "It's getting kind of wacky, isn't it? I thought they had me when those students came on. They were the ones who chased me off the beach the other night, and they spotted me on the beach the day we met. Three times is the charm." She attempted a self-assured laugh, but it sounded forced and nervous, and she knew it. "You'd think people would have more important things to think about than me," she snapped.

"I think about you all the time."

Silence hung between them. "Ev, what am I supposed to say?"

Evan smiled. She'd called him Ev. "You'll think of something appropriate when the time comes." Before she could ask what he meant, he continued, "Listen, sweetheart, I've been watching the weather forecast, and the heat wave doesn't appear to be letting up any time soon. My back-patio sliders are unlocked. Why don't you sleep at my place? It's air-conditioned."

She glanced at her iced-tea glass coated with condensation and puddling onto the table. With no pool and no chance of a dip in the ocean, Holly knew a good offer when she heard one. Still, she hesitated.

"Holly, I probably won't be back for another few nights."

"I'll think about it, thanks."

"Yes. Think about it. Another night in that hot, glorified toolshed or the opportunity to enjoy central air, the Jacuzzi, a balcony overlooking the ocean, and all the ice cream you can eat. Seriously, the house is huge. You wouldn't feel so cramped."

"Who says I feel cramped?"

"You'd have your own room and—"

"I don't think so."

"It's bigger, and air-conditioned. I did tell you it has central air, didn't I?" he teased mercilessly.

"Yes. No."

"Say no if you mean yes, and yes if you mean no."

"No. I mean, yes. Evan, I'm not moving in. We're just asking for— What did you say?"

"See you soon, beautiful."

With the receiver still wedged between his ear and shoulder, Evan reached across his desk and pushed the intercom button. "Tally, would you please come in here?" While he waited for Tally

Evan ran through his conversation with Holly. He didn't like what he'd heard in her voice. The stress was beginning to take its toll on his Glory Girl.

Tally knocked once and walked in, pad and pencil in hand. "Mr. Jamieson, you're not supposed to be here," she began in her no-nonsense voice.

"Me? What about you? It's six forty-five. You ought to be home checking on your cats."

"You know I have parakeets. Did I hear your television a few minutes ago?"

"I was listening to the stock reports."

"You could be watching stock reports on your television in that lovely beach house." She sat down by his desk, put on her glasses, and resumed a professional air. "That Peruvian textile importer could be very well served by Bob Messina and his staff. They can handle L. B. Stoddard too. The only reason Bob paged you—"

"I agree."

Tally opened her mouth and kept it open for a full five seconds. When she finally got control she said, "You do?"

"Yes. We need to do a little reshuffling here. I'm passing this project to Messina."

Tally's eyebrows moved toward each other. "Really?"

Evan stood up and stretched. "Really. We have plenty of good talent around here. I ought to know, I picked them myself. It's time we use them."

She eyed him doubtfully. "Of course. Are you feeling okay?"

"Better than ever, Tally. Why don't you give

Messina and his staff a call and arrange a meeting for us tomorrow. Say, eight A.M.?"

Tally practically bolted for the door. It appeared she wasn't taking any chances that Evan would change his mind.

"Mr. Jamieson?"

"Yes?"

"You'll leave your pager here this time when you go down to Cape Shell, won't you?"

Evan lifted his arm to get a better look at the battery-operated gizmo clipped to his belt. "I'll be taking it. I'm on vacation, not in a coma."

When she left, Evan reached into his shirt pocket and drew out a business card. He tapped it against his thumb, then dropped it on his desk as he reached for the phone. He punched out the numbers and waited.

A male voice with a strong Brooklyn accent answered on the other end. "Hackford Investigative Agency. How can we be of service?"

She could have chosen any bed in his house. She chose his. She'd told herself she'd take a peek at his room before selecting one of the guest bedrooms in which to spend the night. It was probably the sight of his unmade bed, she told herself the following morning, that had made her want to neaten it. Fluffing a pillow seemed innocent enough. If she just hadn't buried her face in it to inhale his scent. She was beginning to act like a love-struck fool, and she knew it, but dropping her clothes beside the king-size bed and slipping, naked, between his sheets seemed so natural at the time. The next morning she promptly washed and dried his bed linens, then purposely ruffled the dressed bed in an attempt to leave it as she'd found it. No harm done. He'd never know, she kept reminding herself, but every inch of her skin tingled with a sweet, raw excitement. The next night she slept there again.

The following afternoon he called to say he was halfway down the parkway and would be arriving in forty-five minutes. Greeting him on his turf, she decided, was asking for trouble. Steeling herself against the heat, she went back to the cottage and began preparing dinner. With every step she promised herself to keep both an emotional and a physical distance from Evan. With every other step she forgot her promise as her excitement grew.

And then he was there.

He announced his arrival by shouting through her screen door, "Surprise."

"Evan, can you manage?" Holding open the door for him, she stepped back as he struggled in with a heavy box.

"Umph," was all he could say as he headed for the kitchen. As he maneuvered the box onto the table, he could only watch her lunge for the wineglass he'd bumped. A flounce of white eyelet encircling her shoulders billowed and took sail across his line of vision.

"Got it!" she exclaimed as they both straightened.

Then he saw the rest of her in the summery sugar-white dress barely skimming her knees and neatly nipped in at the waist with a red-and-yellow sash. That white eyelet flounce pulled below her shoulders set off her amused expression and the sparkle in her green eyes. She'd done something with her hair, too. It was a wonderfully curly mass tied up and spilling out of a green ribbon. Evan's heart thumped hard against his rib cage. Four days was too long to be away from her.

"Hi, beautiful."

"Hello, Evan."

For the space of a heartbeat their gazes met and, just as quickly she looked away. He'd gotten a haircut and had recently shaved. His sunburn had begun darkening to a healthy tan, setting off his blue eyes beautifully. She fought down the urge to reach out and squeeze him. Instead, she brought him an ice-cold beer.

"We're having Mexican food."

"It smells delicious." After a healthy drink, he raised his eyebrows at the box. "Why don't you open that now."

"For me?" she said, as she tore at the ribbons and wrapping. "Oh, Evan." She stepped back and stared at the box. "It's so magnificent."

"No it's not. It's a very big beige air conditioner. Knowing how you love turquoise, I tried getting a turquoise one, but the salesman said they were fresh out." He swiped at his brow, then checked his palms. "Maybe I shouldn't wait until after dinner to install it." He watched her examine the unit as if it were a box containing rare jewels. She opened the plastic envelope and removed the instructions for installation and operation. Carefully. What else, he wondered, did she do so carefully, and with such intense interest? His mind wandered, taking her image with it. He coughed loudly. "Damn, it's hot in here."

Holly looked up, wide eyed with concern. "So

that's why you were inspecting the electrical outlets last week. Is this place wired for such a big
unit?"

"I'm pretty sure. We'll check in a minute."

"I don't know how to thank you," she began.

"I think the jalapeños and hot sauce will take
care of that. Now, tell me what you've been doing
without me for the last four days."

She leaned over and kissed the top of the air
conditioner. "Appreciating the wonders of modern
technology in your house," she said. "Actually,
there isn't much to tell, since you've called me
every day. I called Peaches—"

She stopped herself in midsentence. Evan didn't
need to know she'd called one of the best agencies
in Manhattan to ferret out their newest all-
American models for Stu's appraisal. She'd sent
him half a dozen strawberry blondes last week,
and when Peaches had no more to offer, she'd
arranged for a green-eyed Eurasian and a six-
foot brunette with freckles to show up tomorrow.
Maybe Stu would see that something special, that
unique quality, he believed only Holly possessed.
Maybe. Please, God.

"I mean, I wrote some fund-raising letters for
Lemon Aid. Answered some fan mail. Weeded the
tomatoes. How about you? What did you do?"

"I missed you."

She looked at the unit again.

"I said, I've missed you, Holly." He waited for her
to respond.

She ran her hands over the air conditioner.
"This doesn't look too complicated."

"You're supposed to say 'I missed you too.'"

She stared at him out of the corners of her eyes.

"I checked out all the books in the downstairs study. I ended up reading your copies of *Tom Sawyer*, the Hardy Boys, *Robot Madness*, and the *Salty Dog Joke Book*. Then I glanced through a 1971 copy of *Playboy* I found hidden behind those books. How could I be lonely with that lineup?"

He wanted to hold her close, to press his lips next to those red-gold curls and whisper how crazy he was about her. He couldn't take his eyes from her. "So you made out okay staying at the house?"

"The house was great. I used your VCR and worked out with my aerobics tape. It's been too hot to use it here."

Evan pictured her in a hot-pink leotard and quickly cleared his throat. "We've got to get that unit installed before we both melt."

"Yes. Let's."

In a matter of minutes, with maximum struggling, they'd positioned the air conditioner in a side window of the cottage. "Let's check the circuit breakers. The panel's in a storage room behind your bedroom."

"It is?" She followed him into her room and watched as he dragged a small bureau away from the wall and removed a painting.

"A secret room? Just like in Nancy Drew."

"A secret room, just like in the Hardy Boys," he corrected. Evan opened a short door, hunched his shoulders, and passed through into a dark room. With a little hesitation Holly followed.

Evan steadied her with one hand and pulled the light chain with the other. They stood silent, staring at the contents of the storage room. Crab pots were stacked in one corner, along with coiled

ropes and life preservers. Folding chairs and two
beach umbrellas rested on the floor, and fishing
rods hung from the ceiling.

"It's been so long. God, I loved this place," he
whispered.

"The ultimate secret hideout," commented Holly.

"Oh, yes," he said softly, thoughtfully.

She watched him walk around the room, exam-
ining this, testing that. He laughed quietly and
shook his head now and then, ignoring the heat
and the cramped space.

"What was it like down here at the beach in the
summers? For a boy, I mean?"

He turned toward her, but didn't meet her gaze.
Instead, he stared off, focusing on nothing in
particular. "It was a great place to be a kid,
roaming around town like a pack of puppies.
Crabbing in the bay, surfing in the ocean. And
then, after dinner and before we went to the
boardwalk, we'd all meet here. Some nights we'd
bring our sleeping bags and stay until morning."
His head tilted the tiniest bit. "Summer after
summer. Then one summer . . . well, never mind
that." He looked at her, then reached for the panel
on the circuit breakers.

"Wait. What were you going to say?"

He laughed gently. "Oh, Holly, I don't think you
want to hear that story."

"Sure I do," she whispered, sensing it had to do
with a first love.

He hesitated.

"Oh, go on," she urged. She plunked herself
onto a battered trunk. "We're grown-ups."

"It was a long, long time ago." He sat down
across from Holly on a pile of coiled ropes. "I was

seventeen, and she was almost seventeen. We'd dated that summer, and she was about to go back to—Indiana, I think. We'd had our fill of candied apples and bonfires on the beach. French kissing didn't quite do it, either. So one night I brought her here. She was really a very sweet girl. And as eager as I was to see what lovemaking was all about." He smiled again and shook his head. "I can't believe you want to hear this."

Dust motes danced around his head in the dim light. "I can," she said quietly.

"Well, it was the first time for both of us. We made it through with a minimum of bumbling, as I remember. Afterward I wondered what was going through her mind. I mean, there we were, seventeen and crazy about each other. I had taken precautions, so I wasn't concerned about that. I wanted to know if she'd regretted it. She left for home the next day without us getting a chance to talk much. I spent the rest of the summer wondering if she'd been disappointed, if maybe I'd done it wrong."

Holly was bemused. Evan, doing it wrong? Inconceivable. She'd imagined how it would be to make love with Evan so many times in the last week, and not once had he done anything wrong. "Oh, Evan, I can't believe that."

A bright, amused expression crossed his face. "Really?"

Thank God for the dim light; Holly's face was burning. "I-I mean, uh. Well, that you'd doubted. Actually, forget I said that."

"The hell I will."

"But what happened?" she added quickly.

"I got a letter from her about a month later. She said she still respected me."

"Oh, Evan!"

"No, really. She did. She also said it was the most wonderful night of her life, but that her senior year was starting, and she wanted me to know she was going to start dating."

"Did you keep in touch?"

"No." He stood and reached for her hand. "Care to share anything about yourself with me over dinner?" She looked up at him with wide-eyed surprise, and he knew instantly that she'd misunderstood. "Whoops, don't take that wrong. That's not a question a gentleman should ever ask a lady. I was asking about your current problem. The one that keeps you here."

"I'm going to check on dinner," she announced, pointedly ignoring his question. She lowered her head and walked through to her bedroom.

"And I'm going to find out sooner or later," Evan said to himself as he turned back to the circuit breakers.

"You're either having a heat stroke or an impure thought," Evan said, walking into the room. "Which is it?"

"Both," she said boldly, her eyes meeting his. The table laden with food, drink, and candles separated them, giving each one last physical barrier. Evan's eyes became serious and sensual and his expression lost the humor he'd clung to since entering the cottage.

"Come here," he whispered roughly.

"Oh, Evan." She went into his open arms and let him smother her lips with a kiss.

He eased her off-the-shoulder dress further off her shoulders. "I know, darling, I know."

His breath was hot as he trailed kisses down her neck and onto her shoulders. She took his hand and kissed the knuckle he'd skinned hooking up the air conditioner. "I want so much to trust you—"

"Wait. Stop." He took a step back.

Her eyes shimmered with confusion. "What's wrong?" she asked breathlessly.

"I want you, Holly."

A tiny smile lit her face. "You want to go into the bedroom?"

He shook his head. "Right here." He pointed to the floor. "Or on the table. But I'm not going to. We're not going to make love." He watched her face color. The flames in her cheeks weren't from the heat, or from an unquenched desire to make love. She was flaming with embarrassment. "The reason isn't anything you're thinking."

"How do you know what I'm thinking?" Her eyes pleaded for an explanation.

"Holly, just listen. This is as hard for me as it is for you. You mean too much to me now. No quick tumble, not even an entire night in bed, is going to give me what I want. What I need. What we both need."

"And what do we need?"

"For you to tell me what the hell's going on." He reached out to ease the elastic neckline back up her arms. "Don't get me wrong. This isn't a game of challenge. We're both losers until you share, and until then I'll still be wanting you. Just make it quick, because I'm sure I'm losing brain cells every time we stop." He watched her chin quiver as she stole a glance at his face, then looked away. He felt his resolve weaken as anxiety stole the focus from her eyes. God, how he hated watching her in distress, especially when he'd added to that distress. A part of him wanted to leave, to walk outside that gate out there and breathe in the clear, uncomplicated sea air. But he wanted her with him when he did it.

He held her chair and, murmuring thanks, she took it.

"The guacamole has a tomato in it from your garden," she said, trying hard to infuse the simple statement with importance. "I haven't used any chemical repellants on those plants, I want you to know." She offered him a platter of enchiladas. "I picked off those nasty-looking critters by hand. Of course, I've had plenty of time. . . ." Her gaze rose slowly from the platter of food to meet his. "I'm not complaining."

He took the platter and helped himself to a generous portion. "Of course not. Could you pass the sour cream? Thanks. By the way, have you ever been up on the boards for Fiesta Fantasy Night?"

Holly dragged a tortilla chip through her guacamole. "No. They've only had it for the last five years, and I was always working, it seemed. Last year I was out in Tucson with my parents. Have you ever been to Fiesta Fantasy Night?"

"A few years back, right after my divorce, a couple of friends dragged me to it kicking and screaming. It's a lot like Mardi Gras. Have you ever been to Mardi Gras in New Orleans?"

She nodded.

He smiled slowly. Of course she had. She'd probably been to *Carnaval* in Rio. But all that didn't matter. What he really wanted to know was if she'd ever made love on the beach in the moonlight. He inhaled sharply. "Then you can picture it. Bands scattered all over the boardwalk, people dancing to rock and roll or polka music or whatever they're hearing inside their own heads. The smell of fried everything hangs in the air." He took a sip of sangria. "But the best part of all is, everyone is dressed in some kind of costume. Sounds like fun, doesn't it?"

"Sure does. It's next week, isn't it? Next Saturday?"

"Next Saturday," he confirmed.

"Maybe next year . . ." She placed her elbows on the table and rested her chin in the cups of her hands.

Evan winked. "Pass the salsa."

Six

She had to hand it to him; he certainly had a vivid imagination, and no small amount of courage to present this idea to her.

"You said you had a perfectly innocent reason for asking me up to your bedroom. And this is it? This is what you've been so secretive about for the last week? This is why you left weeding the tomatoes all to me?" Holly planted both hands on her hips and paced in front of Evan. "Strolling the boardwalk on Fiesta Fantasy Night is the craziest idea I've ever heard. You know Dennis Cracci will be up there taping, and so will a bunch of other reporters. The whole reason to go there is to be seen. Be stared at. Be found out." She sank into a rattan chair and folded her arms. "Listen, why don't we just stay here and watch it on local cable?"

Evan stood his ground. If she didn't accept this idea, he didn't know what he was going to do to get her out. He couldn't count the times in this last week together that he'd offered to take her, in the dark of night, for a drive. She'd always refused. Well, she wasn't going to refuse tonight. "I shouldn't have to remind you that many of the proceeds are going to children's charities around the state."

"Don't try making me feel guilty. It won't work."

He held out the suit. "But this will. Trust me."

She motioned with both hands. "That outfit couldn't possibly disguise me. You're dressed in the same thing, and I recognize you. Let's just forget it."

"Not so fast. There's more to the disguise than what you see here." He twirled the linen suit for her inspection. "Humor me and try it on." Wagging his finger, he smiled that devastating smile.

When he headed for the bathroom Holly shook her head, stood up, and blithely followed. "Lord, you're determined, but it won't work. Costumes never do. I always knew everyone on Halloween."

Ignoring her protests, Evan hung the suit on the hook behind the door, ripped off its plastic cover, and stepped back. "Note the design here." He ran his hand over the garment like any good suit salesman. "Guaranteed to hide every gorgeous curve of—"

"Evan Jamieson, you don't know everything."

"I know you slept in my bed when I was away."

Before she could stop and think she responded, "How did you know that?"

"I didn't. Not until you admitted it just now. Aren't you going to ask me why I thought you had?"

"No. Look, I'll try this on," she answered, desperate to avoid his playful look. "You're the only one who'll ever see me in this." Evan's idea was insane, but if trying the clothes on would allow her to escape his question and end his determination to take her out in public, she'd try them on. She waved him out, closed the door, and quickly pulled off her shorts. Certain she'd be back in the rest of her clothes soon enough, she didn't bother removing her silky black T-shirt. Stepping into the full-cut trousers, she pulled them up and fastened them. One of the bathroom walls was fully mirrored, and she turned to look at what she'd put on so far.

"Hey," she shouted through the door. "How'd you know my size?"

"I've been studying your body from every angle."

She smiled into the mirror before reaching for the jacket. Noting the label, she winced. He'd obviously spared no expense for this hopeless idea, she realized as she pulled on the designer piece. "Just who are—who were we supposed to be?"

"Glad you asked. I thought with the mustaches and cigars—"

Holly yanked the door open. "Mustaches and cigars?"

Evan, sporting a newly applied mustache, round tortoiseshell glasses, and a slicked-back hairdo, breezed into the spacious bathroom.

Holly gave a little shriek. "I can't believe it. I swear, for a split second I didn't know it was you."

He rubbed his hands together. "Great. That's the reaction we want. I thought beards would be too itchy, especially since you've never had one."

"Gee, thanks. I've never had a mustache either."

"You will in a moment." He backed her up and sat her down on the rim of the whirlpool tub, then dropped the toilet lid and sat down facing her. "About that little hormone problem . . ." He pulled a box from his pocket, opened the kit, and set it on the sink. "Voilà!"

Holly couldn't help smiling as she watched Evan push up his sleeves. Unscrewing the small tube of adhesive, he studied her upper lip like a doctor preparing for surgery. Even if they weren't going up on the boardwalk, even if she was stuck behind his fence for another night, his boyish charm and energy promised definite mental escape. Perhaps that's what he'd been planning all along. He couldn't really be expecting her to leave the safety of his compound. Her train of thought was smoothly derailed by the sensation of Evan's thighs as they pressed against her knees. He'd leaned in to stare at her face and a mix of images vied for first place in Holly's thoughts.

Two kids playing dress up . . .

Evan's thighs pressing against hers . . .

The tub's cool rim beneath her fingers as she strengthened her grip . . .

Evan snipping at her auburn mustache with manicure scissors . . .

Beneath his own mustache his lips pursed in concentration . . .

She was melting.

Holly swallowed hard and studied the design on the shower curtain. After an endless moment she spoke. "Who did you say you were supposed to be?"

"Reginald Q. Coxswain here, argyle socks salesman from Kennebunkport." The exaggerated New England accent sent Holly into a fit of chortling.

He pushed his glasses above his forehead. "Ready?"

Holly pressed her lips together and gave a quick nod.

"Lean in so I can put this thing on you." Evan dabbed at her upper lip with a dry washcloth, laid it slowly over their thighs, then lifted the tube of adhesive. "Don't move. I've never put a mustache on anyone but me."

Holly's eyes widened as a tickling line of adhesive was applied above her mouth. "What?" she asked through clenched jaws. "You haven't done this? Ever?"

He recapped the tube and, without taking his eyes from hers, tossed the tube over his shoulder and into the sink. "Don't move . . . not a muscle." Her lips quivered as she fought back laughter. "If you move those lips one more time, I'll kiss you."

"I'm trying, I swear I'm trying," she said before a fit of laughter overtook her. Whatever happened tonight, she knew she'd remember the laughter the most. The giggling, outrageous fun he'd given her was already a treasured memory. She took a deep breath, held it, then let it out slowly. "Okay, I'm okay." But she wasn't. "You look so funny in that mustache and those glasses and your hair . . . and when y-you—" she began, then fell against his chest and burst out laughing again. As she slid to the floor, he began laughing too.

How long he'd wanted this! To see her joyful. To see her free of her burdens, if only for an evening. He watched her sitting on the floor, her head resting on the rim of the tub as she held her sides. Wouldn't she be fun to have at his side out there in the world, sharing life's pleasures! Or, just the two of them alone laughing intimately at a shared secret. Hell, he wanted her close even when she cried, because he loved her. With all his heart he loved her.

After a few minutes Holly wiped her eyes. "I'm sorry. It's your mustache. You twitch it every time you get close to me."

Evan shoved a hand through his hair, then pinched his nose. It wasn't time to tell her he loved her, not yet. "Perhaps I should have planned on matching straitjackets." He helped her back to the rim of the tub. "Seriously, now, before your adhesive dries."

"Yes, sir."

Supporting her jawline with his thumb, he kept her face tilted upward, and her gaze locked with his. His gaze drifted lower and, after careful positioning, he gently patted the mustache in place.

"How do I look?" Her speech was slurred as she forced her face to remain still. It wasn't easy with Evan's face inches from her and his fingertips gently holding the sides of her face.

"Like someone I once refused to fly out of Colombia. Be still."

With him around she found she was never still. She either wanted to run to him or from him. Right now she wanted to move about four inches closer, but people in hell wanted ice water, and that didn't mean they could have it. She sighed.

His fingertips lingered near the edges of the mustache, then began tracing a tantalizing pattern on her lips. She eyed him suspiciously. "What are you doing?"

"Checking for symmetry. Don't talk. You'll come unglued."

You got that right, she thought, as she stared at the wide lapels of his light linen jacket. Coming unglued was exactly how she felt. With him so near, so determined, and so much fun, she didn't look forward to telling him all his carefully laid plans weren't going to work. His intentions were admirable, but how could a fake mustache and a baggy suit shield her from the crowds? For that matter, how could Evan? Well, she might as well get it over with. "Can I look now?"

Evan checked his watch and eased away from her. "Sure." He stood up, then offered her his hand.

"By the way, who was I supposed to be?" she asked taking his hand.

"Holly, meet Carlos, the emerald salesman. Up close and personal." He pointed to the mirrored wall beside them.

With more interest than she wanted him to see Holly stood up and turned. She was speechless. The image staring back at her was startling. She lifted up her hair, twisted it tightly at the crown and studied the effect. "I—I look like Uncle Richard. Ev, I look just like my uncle Richard." For the first time that evening she began to see the possibility of a night out. A real night out. Letting her hair fall back around her shoulders, she turned around to Evan. "Oh, my. This is amazing. Really."

"Pull up your hair again, and we'll try it with the hat." He left the bathroom, and she followed.

"You got us hats too?" She caught her reflection

in his dresser mirror, lifted her hair once again, and waited. "Hurry."

He returned from his walk-in closet wearing a hat and carrying another. "Why? Are we going somewhere?" Standing behind her he placed the woven straw hat on her head. Their eyes met briefly in the mirror. "Kind of like a straw fedora," he explained, standing back.

Tipping it forward to angle slightly over one eye, Holly studied her altered image. There was no denying it. Evan had succeeded in obliterating most every recognizable feature of the Glory Girl. "My own parents wouldn't know me," she whispered. Her gaze suddenly connected with his in the mirror. "Do you really think this will work?"

"I think . . . Carlos the emerald salesman knows how to fill out a T-shirt."

She glanced at the very feminine line her breasts made through the silky black top under the jacket, then sighed loudly. "What are we going to do with them?"

His hands slipped under her jacket and around her waist, then his fingers did a tickling walk halfway up her ribs. "I thought you'd never ask," he replied in his best lecherous drawl. Before she could react, he withdrew his hands and buttoned her jacket. "Come on, Carlos, we've got some deceiving to do. Let's get the hell out of here and have some fun."

Holly shook her head as she continued to stare into the mirror, but she was smiling. "I didn't say I was going."

"Well, say you're going and let's go."

"Evaaaan?" Her whine was grating and entirely theatrical.

"Yes?"

"Can I pleeeease wear the glasses?"

Evan sighed, and with elaborate exaggeration reluctantly pulled off the glasses. "Oh, all right, but I get to light my cigar."

She took the glasses and slipped them on. Thoroughly pleased with her look, she slipped her hands into the deep pockets of her trousers and twisted her head from side to side.

"Great," Evan said in a stagy whisper, "while you're falling in love with Carlos, they're probably running out of beer and pizza up there. Are you about ready?"

"Evan?" She leaned in closer to the mirror and studied the edges of her mustache. "These don't come off like the ones in the movies, right? I mean, we don't actually have to rip them off, do we?"

"I hope not."

Holly pulled her hands from her pockets and turned slowly toward him. "What? You are joking, aren't you?"

Evan forced an innocent look onto his face. "Well, the last time I had a mustache, I'd actually grown it myself. That's an interesting story. You see, my fraternity had this bet—"

Crushing his lapels in her fists, she pulled him close. "I don't care about your fraternity. I care about my upper lip, and if I'll have one in the morning."

He pulled his pager from his belt, looked at it for a second, then tossed it onto his bed. "Carlos, baby, trust me."

"Hmmmm." Without letting go of him, she looked over her shoulder toward the mirror. The disguise he'd concocted was incredible. "Maybe I should braid my hair and pin—Ev, what are you doing?"

He'd wrapped one arm around her waist, lifted her onto his hip and was carrying her out of the room. "Picking up my date."

Holly pressed her thighs against Evan's as the little moped whizzed its way through block after block of parked cars.

"Relax," he instructed, "I took the training wheels off this about twenty years ago."

Clutching her hat brim with one hand, she held on to Evan's belt with the other. As the bike took each curve Holly molded herself tightly to his back. She could smell anticipation in the thick sea air.

"We'll chain this behind the Cape Shell Café," Evan called back to her. He maneuvered the moped through a scraggly group of teenagers, drove into a parking lot, and slipped off into a dark alleyway.

Bumping and lurching, the moped coughed and stopped. Evan shrugged and patted the gas tank. "Cheated death again. I've been working on old Greased Lightnin' all week. She hasn't been on these streets for years. Of course, neither have I."

Holly's fingers lingered near the hard muscles of Evan's stomach. "It was wonderful." Her cheek still rested against his back, and in a moment of blissful honesty, she gave in to her desire to hold him a second longer.

Evan covered her hand with his and gave it a gentle squeeze. "This'll be your first evening out in weeks. Are you ready?"

Holly disentangled herself from Evan, swung

her leg over the moped, and walked around in front of it. She was all tingly from the ride. Or was it from clinging to Evan, sharing every vibration with him, every intimate bump, every inch of his hard, perfectly muscled back? She coughed once. "If my hair stays tucked in, I'm ready." Making the perfunctory attempt to smooth out the wrinkles in her linen trousers, she adjusted her glasses in his rearview mirror, then looked at him with a devilish smile. "So, what's a guy do around here for a good time?"

He swung his leg over the bike, toed down the kickstand, and leaned the bike at a secure angle. He took off his fedora and dipped his head close to her face. His mustache brushed against her ear when he whispered roughly, "Eat."

Holly inhaled. "I smell french fries and malt vinegar."

He grabbed her hand. "Follow that smell," he commanded as they raced toward the ramp.

Unable to keep his eyes from her even if he wanted to, he was still watching as they crested the entrance ramp. She opened her mouth and stuck out her tongue like a little child.

"You can taste the air. Go ahead," she dared him. "Do it."

He stuck out his tongue. She was right. He tasted the salty, slightly metallic sea air. "You're right. Over thirty years and it never changes."

She shook her head and laughed, her eyes sparkling with mirth. The disguise had bolstered her confidence beyond his wildest hopes. That was all he wanted, he told himself. To get her out, to set some part of her free, and then to selfishly enjoy her. The danger inherent in his plan seemed minimal at the moment. They were receiving no more and no less attention than anyone else.

Without warning, Holly tugged his hand, then plunged into the crowd. And he was right beside her, fingers laced tight with hers, shouldering through the thick of it with her. All the smells were there, and the sounds too. Music blared from several sources, and shrieks of laughter laced with shouted salutations shot through the gaudily lit night. Costumes ranged from black leather motorcycle gear complete with chains to sequined bikinis decorated in neon-pink plumage. But the reality of the moment, his moment, centered on Holly. She was having the time of her life.

"Way up there," she shouted. "That's Tessie's French Fry Palace. Come on." She dragged him through the crowds and past a funnel-cake concession and an Italian water-ice cart. "Annie and I worked here one summer," she announced as they reached Tessie's. "Cleanest grease on the boards."

He paid for paper cones of fries while she sprinkled them with malt vinegar. They plowed through the crowd toward the railing overlooking the beach. While Holly breathed in the sea air, Evan watched her. Colored lights were reflecting off the water along with a trail of moonlight, but they paled next to her radiant smile. He reached out to touch her cheek.

"Is it coming off?" she asked, pressing a knuckle to her mustache.

He pursed his lips and shook his head to reassure her. "I think it's growing there now."

Her throaty scream was lost in the noise around

them, but her carefully aimed french fry hit him on the shoulder. "That was not funny."

As an act of atonement he moved closer and dropped one of his fries into her cone. "Sorry."

But she'd already forgotten the silly scare. "Why," she asked through a mouthful of fries, "does something so good have to be so bad for you?"

"Shh! You'll take the fun out of it if you have to analyze." There was a break in the crowd, and he motioned for them to walk. "WCSB is in that van, and I think they're playing old Stones music. Can you hear it?"

They tossed the paper cones into an already overflowing trash can and made their way toward a roped-off stage. A dance contest was in progress, and Holly's shoulders and hips were already making time with the music. She couldn't contain the rhythm inside her, he realized, as he watched her give in to the music. Mustache, hat, baggy suit—it wasn't working. There was a woman in there, anyone could see that. But no one could tell she was the Glory Girl. His girl. He lit his cigar and proudly watched his dream become a reality. The whole boardwalk seemed to be moving to the hard-rock music, but Holly, alone, moved Evan.

Still staring at the dancers, she attempted to carry on a dialogue with him. "Don't even think about asking me to dance. I'm happy right where I am." She adjusted the bridge of her glasses with one perfectly manicured nail. "Oh, did you see that one? A Klingon dancing with a Vulcan. Pretty kinky if you ask me."

"Carlos! We have to—"

A stream of slick chatter rolled off the tongue of

someone nearby, interrupting Evan. "Hey, you two. How ya doing tonight? Can we talk to you for a moment? We'd like to interview you for our show, *Entertainment-4-You.* Toby, roll tape. So, just who do we have here?"

Holly's body stopped swaying before her hands stopped clapping. The voice was entirely too familiar. Evan's hand slipped between hers and closed firmly. Her eyes slid sideways, and her stomach flip-flopped. Dennis Cracci had a microphone several inches from Evan's face. She looked at Evan.

Evan looked at her. "Ready?"

Cracci leaned in closer. "Speak up, we couldn't get that."

"Reginald Q. Coxswain, argyle socks salesman from Kennebunkport, you dip," said Evan as he slipped into the crowd with Holly close beside him.

"Do you think he recognized me? Do you?" she whispered frantically.

"If he did, I don't think he'd be bothering that gorilla in the Hawaiian shirt. Do you?"

For the next hour they stayed clear of the roped-off dancing area near the radio van. Instead, they rode the Ferris wheel and Poe's Pendulum, stumbled through Barnie's Hall of Mirrors, and drove separate bumper cars until Holly thought her teeth would shake loose.

"Take me someplace where I can be still," she pleaded over the battered pink hood of her car.

When they were out on the boards again he waited while she wiped perspiration from her forehead and readjusted her hat. "Holly, you must be a holy terror on the parkway."

He was teasing her, and she loved it. "How can you say that? I'm a great driver. I—" She stopped talking when she noticed several people staring at her. "Evan?"

Evan had noticed, too. "Keep walking and don't look at them. Come on." In the hope that it would reassure her, he rested his hand against the small of her back. "Are you okay?"

"Fine. Maybe they're just admiring your mustache work." She touched her upper lip then winked at him. "I can't believe I've lived all these years without one of these."

He pulled her closer. "Happy you came?"

"Yes. Very happy." She smiled. "Very, very happy," she whispered.

He spoke first, breaking the crystal moment of intimacy they'd created amid the throngs of people. "The night's still young. Let's go."

They were soon moving along the edge of the boardwalk close to the games. Bells were ringing, balloons were popping, and dollar bills were disappearing over the counters. "You're safe. No one's following. See, everyone's interested in bouncing rubber frogs onto lily pads and bursting water balloons."

Holly stopped. "Oh, no! Not again," she mumbled.

Not ten feet away stood Dennis Cracci. He was having his makeup retouched and his lines read to him, and several groupies were entertaining him with their adoring stares.

The flow of the crowd prevented him from backing away from the troublesome reporter. "What'll we do?" Holly whispered to him as they stared at Dennis Cracci.

Evan pulled her around to the closest counter, shoved a dollar bill into her hand and slapped one down on a numbered square himself. "Play," he said pleasantly. "Just don't turn around."

The barker droned, a wheel spun, and the other players pounded their fists on the counter. A triumphant shout went up as the wheel clicked to a stop.

"I want the blue one," someone shouted. Someone had won a prize, but Holly was too miserable to see what it was.

Holly pulled down the brim of her hat until it rested on the top of her glasses. "Is he gone?"

"Not yet. He's taping a line of dancers. Once they get out of here, we'll be fine." He slapped another bill on the counter and slid it under her hand. "Keep playing."

Same drone. Same clickcty-clack spin. Same pounding. Same misery.

"Holly," Evan whispered. "Get ready."

The crowd groaned. Holly looked at Evan. "What? I can't hear you."

A beefy hand covered hers. "Hey, young fella. Looks like you won. What color you want your prize in?"

Evan looked up first. "Uh-oh." He pointed across the counter. "Take a look at what you've won Carlos."

She shoved back her hat and, for the first time, looked up at the wheel and what was behind it. The entire back wall was papered in Glory Girl posters. Red ones. Gold ones. Blue ones. Row after row of plastic-wrapped cylinders were stacked beneath the display. Glittering letters proclaimed number seventeen would win all three. Holly slowly turned her head to look down the counter at the other players of Glory Girl Roulette. Some had already won the coveted prize and were placing their bets again.

She looked at Evan. *This couldn't be happening to her.*

"It's a hard choice," said the barker. "How about a red one?" He rolled the plastic-wrapped cylinder across the counter, and Holly reached to stop it. "Place your—hey, look. That's that guy from TV. Hey, Dennis! Over here."

Clutching the poster to her side, Holly stepped back. *This simply wasn't happening.* Someone jostled her, and suddenly a line of dancers separated her from Evan. Extra dancers had connected with the line, thickening it by twos and threes, and now she could barely see Evan. In the confusion one dancer knocked Holly's hat over her glasses and nose. She made a frantic grab for the hat and ended up knocking it completely off. In one of those surreal moments, Holly watched the hat descend toward the boards, then stop in mid air.

"Got it," proclaimed a surprised voice.

She looked up. Dennis Cracci's grin froze as he watched the Glory Girl's red-gold hair spill down around her shoulders. "Holly Hamilton," he whispered in disbelief.

"Trust me." It was Evan's voice she was hearing now. This wasn't a nightmare. It was worse, much worse. She was numb, crazy, and having auditory hallucinations all at the same time.

"Give me the poster, Holly." Evan peeled her frozen fingers from the rolled poster and held it high in the air. "Free Glory Girl poster," he shouted as he whirled it over his head. "A free red one." He pitched it spearlike over a sea of reaching hands. The crowd turned on its collective heel and ran toward the opposite side of the boardwalk.

Dennis Cracci looked as though he was about to have a fit. "Toby, roll tape. Toby, forget the poster. Roll tape. Roll tape."

One look at Holly, and Evan knew she was completely stunned by her discovery. She was still staring openmouthed at Dennis Cracci. Evan cringed at the outcome of his carefully planned evening. She'd never trust him again, but that was far down the list of things to deal with. Right now he had to get her safely away. Evan spoke as evenly as he could. "Holly? Sweetheart, please."

Holly reached for Evan's outstretched hand, and together they made a dash for the nearest ramp. They never stopped running until they were in the dark alley beside the moped. In moments Evan was shouting a prayer of thanks as the little engine roared to life. Holly hopped on, and they shot out of the alley, leaving a gasping Dennis Cracci on the curb holding Holly's hat and a microphone.

Twenty minutes later Evan turned the moped into the parking lot near the pavilion, drove as close to the beach path as he could, and cut the engine. Once Holly was off the bike, Evan got off and untied the rolled-up blanket behind the seat. "This way," he said, then walked up the path through the dunes to the beach. Holly put the fake glasses in her pocket, rolled up her trouser legs, removed her shoes, and followed closely behind.

He spread the blanket, then indicated with a wave of his hand for Holly to sit. For several seconds only the rush of the waves could be heard. Finally Holly sat down, crossed her legs Indian style, and leaned back on her elbows.

"Moon's awfully bright tonight," she said, attempting to reach out to some less tense plane where they could talk.

"Yes." He paced before her, rubbing the back of his neck.

"This is where I first saw you. Where you first saw me."

"Yes."

"Are you very mad?"

Evan pulled off his hat and threw it down beside Holly. "Yes, dammit. Aren't you?"

"About what? We're safe now."

Evan dropped to his knees. "It was all my idea. I'm the one who caused your catatonic reaction to Cracci. Now he knows you're in town." He reached for her shoulders. "I'm so sorry about all of this. What an arrogant, presumptuous son of a—"

"Evan, stop it right there."

"I mean it, Holly. When you saw the posters and then that damned reporter—I wouldn't blame you if you never wanted to see me again."

"There's no need to apologize."

"Annie said you thought the poster was kind of cute after you thought about it. When I saw your expression back there when you saw those posters, I realized she had it all wrong."

Holly pressed her hand over his mouth. "No, she didn't." She watched his eyebrows arch in surprise, but he said nothing. "Thank you for taking me out, for giving me tonight. I haven't laughed so loud and so long in months. Maybe years. Even if things got a little crazy there at the end, well . . . as someone once said, 'You're the best time I ever had.'" Holly dropped both her hands to his knees. "I mean it, Evan. Tonight was wonderful."

Moonlight shimmered in her eyes as she looked up into his. Here she was, all fresh and dewy. All his. She wasn't lying; he could always tell when she was. She never ceased to amaze him, he thought as the tension began uncoiling in his chest and his emotions began to center on her once again. "You know, the last person with a mustache I kissed was my aunt Martha. It wasn't a pleasant experience. I think it's about time we take these off." He reached for the corner of his mustache, and she started to reach for hers.

She stopped, then grabbed his shirt. "Wait! Is this going to hurt?"

"Probably. Let's try it this way." He reached for the edge of hers, and she reached for his. "Ready?"

"Not really."

Blatantly ignoring her cowardice, he started counting. "Three, two, one."

Rrrrrip. Several seconds of silence. She dropped his mustache, then quickly fingered the space above her own lip. "How do you feel?"

"Like I did a second ago. I still want to kiss you. Come here."

Waves pounded on the hard-packed sand as she raised up on her knees and let him gather her up against the length of him. She was soft and warm and in his arms, sighing his name. Desire shot through him, and he suddenly had to experience her with all his senses. He slanted his mouth to nibble at her lips, to lick inside when she opened them with a gasp.

"Touch me," he whispered against her mouth. She pulled his shirt from his waistband and, dragging her nails delicately across his torso, slid the shirt higher. Her boldness provided the impetus for him to speak again. "I take back what I said about waiting. Share your secret with me when you can, but, God, Holly, let me love you tonight."

He could feel her stiffen, then slowly straighten up. Flattening her palms against his chest, she pushed away as a helpless look of desperation clouded her features. Tears were welling up in her eyes, and Evan could feel his own throat tightening. "What can I do? Just tell me what to do," he demanded in a fierce whisper. "I'll move the moon. All you have to do is ask."

Once she told him everything would change. She rubbed her face and sat back on the blanket. "I never wanted you to get involved, but you are now. It isn't right keeping this from you any longer." She opened her mouth to continue, but nothing came out. She tried again. "This is so hard. Just give me a minute."

"Whatever you need."

She wrapped her arms around her knees and rested her chin on them. Her instinct for survival kicked in, replaying the same familiar scenario as she stared across the watery trail of moonlight. Run. Escape. Hide. Fly away over the platinum pathway to the moon. Away from here, away from Evan and the impossible situation she was in. She blew out through pursed lips. That was fantasy, and this was reality. Evan, who was so many things, was her friend. Now he would be her confidant.

She twisted her head toward him. "I never really

thought that poster was tacky. If I hated anything about it, it was that I never had any control over it. I placed my trust in Stu and literally got caught with my pants down for doing it. In one unguarded moment my carefully crafted all-American image was shattered all to hell. Anyone who looks at that poster can see I was shocked that my photo was being taken. Twenty-six-year-old responsible women do not let things like that happen. Stu stole what public credibility I had, and it's going to get worse."

"I don't understand—"

"Evan, some people are saying there's going to be a second poster. Those rumors are correct. It's only a matter of time."

"Another poster?" he repeated. "What do you mean?"

"I mean Stu kept that camera clicking longer than I told you. His talent, besides photography, lies in manipulation. He says if I don't come back to work for him, he's going to market this other poster. I don't think he's bluffing."

"Holly, how bad can this second one be?"

"I don't know. But it doesn't have to be much worse for me to lose the chance to be on the board of Lemon Aid. They won't want me representing a children's charity while I appear to be offering anatomy lessons to anyone with ten dollars."

"All that doesn't matter to me."

"But it does to me. Lemon Aid is the one organization that I believe I can make a difference with." She pushed her hair behind her ears and stared at the water again. The tide was starting in. The world was still spinning toward another day; it hadn't ended yet. She spoke softly. "I want children of my own someday. What will they say about their mother? And how will I answer them?" She shook her head. "I'm babbling. I'm sorry." Her hands balled into fists, and she shook them by her face. "I'm doing everything I can to end this, but I swear, if the second poster comes out, I'll quit before I'll ruin Lemon Aid's name."

Her hands opened in a gesture of hopelessness. "Then there's you. What's it going to do to your business if you're linked with me, with the peek-aboo, brainless, bare-butt bimbo?"

When he didn't respond, she stood up, took off her jacket, and tossed it beside him. "Now you know." She shoved her hands into the deep pockets of her trousers and walked away from him and toward the frothy, meandering edge of the ocean.

Evan stared at the place on the blanket where she had been. Business wasn't what bothered him. It was her comment about wanting children someday. He'd always wanted children, too, but since his divorce he'd suppressed that desire because the right woman had never come along. There was always the future, he'd tell himself when he felt the longing spreading in his chest after a conversation with a niece or nephew. When Annie's kids hugged him. When he flew children, their faces rosy with the excitement of an airplane trip and a pilot who talked to them. He plowed both hands through his hair. The future had arrived, and so had the right woman. He was more certain of that now than ever. And she'd finally trusted him to tell him everything.

She was walking back and forth along the beach. Moonlight outlined her in liquid silver, and the mild sea breeze lifted and tossed the ends of her hair draping her downcast face. Smiling to himself, he stood up.

"Holly?"

She looked up to see his open arms.

"We'll deal with your ex. Together we'll turn this thing around, Holly, I swear we will."

She came toward him, but stopped short of his reach.

He beckoned with his fingers. "Come on, a little closer. That's it."

The hard lump inside her chest began breaking up. There was no denying the compelling attraction any longer and she went to him.

"I want you, Holly. Right here, right now." Her gaze locked with his as his hands slipped beneath the edge of her top. He lifted it up and off of her. A breeze blew up from the water, but she barely recognized it. Every sensation she was experiencing seemed to come from Evan.

"Take off your trousers, Holly."

Unzipping them, she allowed them to fall and stepped out of them. She watched his fingers trace the lacy edge of her black satin teddy. A hot river of pleasure streamed from her center to follow his hand. He circled the red rosette nestled between her breasts, then dragged his finger over the stiffening peak of one nipple and down to the high-cut hip.

"Did you put this on for me?"

Until that moment she would have denied that intention to God Himself. "Yes."

He smiled that devastating smile, and she thought she'd die with pleasure. He looked her up and down, his eyes heavy with desire. "And will you take it off for me?"

"Yes," she whispered, her voice thick with the anticipation of where this was leading.

"Take it off for me," he repeated, his nostrils flaring. The bright moonlight did little to soften the naked want in his face.

She slipped one satin strap, then the other, from her shoulders. The lace-edged cups shifted lower, revealing tight peaks of rosy flesh. As she lowered the silky top, she looked up to meet his gaze, her full, high breasts milk white in the moonlight. In her moment of hesitation he peeled off his shirt, then unhooked his trousers and removed them along with his briefs. He was ready, she realized with a deeply feminine satisfaction. She slid the teddy further down her body, along the deep curve of her waist to the gentle flare of her hips, then stopped, staring at him again.

"Let me do it," he said, kneeling before her and hooking his thumbs inside the lingerie. He tugged it lower, kissing the flat plane of her belly, nuzzling her hip, then stroking her tight, sleek thighs. Holly grabbed his shoulders, steadying herself against the onslaught of sensation. He moved his mouth lower until she thought she'd scream with wanting him. Their kiss was joy and desire, hunger and love, want and need. He pulled her with him to the blanket, then parted her legs and levered himself into the cradle of her womanhood. Poised above her, he drew in the sea air and the scent of her.

"Holly?"

She understood the unspoken question, the protocol of new lovers, that one last moment to turn it all around. And she blessed him for the gesture. Blessed him with a soul-searing kiss.

With a kitten-soft moan of surrender, she grasped his thighs and welcomed him deep inside. Then he was thrusting inside her, surging, stroking, filling her with spiraling pleasure. The moon hid behind a cloud as she arched to answer each thrust, each forbidden command he whispered in the dark night.

"Say you're mine," he managed in a ragged voice, slowly reining himself in.

How had she lived without him? Without his love? Without his loving? "I am." She pressed her hands against the hollow of his back, forcing him to fill her again. And then the surging, stroking rhythm quickened until Holly felt herself shattering into a thousand pieces of glittering pleasure.

He followed her through the star shower of sensation, slipping away inside her intimate embrace to be with her. To be. Sated, complete, and loved, he held her in his arms listening to the sea, to their hearts, and to the sweetest sound of all, Holly's voice.

"I'm yours."

Seven

After smearing extra mayonnaise on his second ham sandwich, Evan piled on thick tomato slices and pickle chips. Smiling broadly to himself when it didn't fall apart, he carefully lifted the sandwich toward his mouth. Inches before he got there he asked, "Sure I can't make one of these for you?"

"No, thank you." The afterglow from their recent lovemaking had Holly feeling energized and not the least bit hungry. Dangling her legs over Evan's kitchen counter, she leaned back against a cabinet. Watching him eat his sandwich was all she wanted to keep her content.

Putting her trust in Evan was the right thing to do. Together they would come up with a plan to end Stu's farce. The only things left to fight tonight were the dreamy smiles stealing across her face. And wasn't that champagne zinging through her veins again?

"I like it when you call me Glory Girl. Did you know that?"

"Yes." He watched as she smiled more to herself than to him. "Any more questions, Glory Girl?" he asked before taking another healthy bite.

"Uh-huh. About your appetite. Where'd you get it? From all that sea air?" She leaned sideways on the counter, planting her elbows inches from his plate. "Or zipping around on your moped?" she asked playfully.

He shook his head and mumbled through a mouthful, "Exercise. On the beach." He winked at her before chugging his orange juice from the carton.

The phone rang, then died on the second ring. Wrong number that time, he supposed, but the telephone always seemed to be lurking, ready to invade. He shook his head and frowned at Holly. "I can't get away from the telephone entirely, but I think we ought to get you out of Cape Shell for a while. We could let Annie know and be out of here early tomorrow."

She pictured a secluded hideaway in the Poconos or down in the Caribbean. An Eden of a place where they could savor their newfound intimacy. September was still a few weeks away. "Suggestions?"

"How about my apartment in New York? We'll probably be able to keep a better handle on everything up there and still have all the privacy we want."

She gave him a sad little smile. "I'll miss this place, but you're right. Too many close calls here lately. I hate to see you spend the rest of your vacation in Manhattan during August."

"Alone with each other." He gave her his best wicked smile.

He was wearing his linen trousers, but had removed his shirt and jacket after arriving home from the beach. Her eyes strayed from his gorgeously muscled arms, across the curly mat of dark hair covering his chest, and all the way down to the darker whorl of hair circling his navel. Figuring out solutions, he'd told her once, was what he did best. Actually that wasn't what he did best. How could he be fantastically sexy and yet so practical, all at the same time, she wondered?

He wiped his mouth, then looked at her. "Getting back to the problem with your ex, I think negotiating is the way to resolve it, Holly. You'll have to go into it prepared with as much information as you can get."

Her gaze drifted slowly back to his face. The last thing she'd wanted to talk about was Stu, but Evan was right. The sooner she concluded this awful mess, the better. "You mean I'll have to get Stu to compromise?"

He nodded once. "Unless . . ." He slipped a pickle chip into his mouth and chewed thoughtfully.

"Unless what?"

"We know Stu is willing to give up the negative to get you back to work. What we don't know is what he's not willing to give up. He'll be demanding you model for him unless you can counter with something big—say, something he doesn't want known."

Holly sat up again. "You mean like something illegal?"

"Or embarrassing." He raised his hand. "Come on. First thing that pops into your mind about him. Say it."

She shrugged. "Like . . . he's a pack rat. He saves everything."

"Hmmm." Evan gave her a doubtful look, then wiped the bread crumbs from his hands. "First impressions are usually quite telling. Was that your first impression of him?"

She shook her head as she watched him open the freezer and search through cartons of frozen food. "Determination. No, I take that back. Manipulation. I told you how he got me to work for him." She shifted for a more comfortable position on the counter. "I was naive and gullible." She fell silent and began a laborious examination of her nails. "Very naive and extremely gullible."

Evan walked away from the open freezer compartment and, smiling indulgently, lifted her chin and dropped a soft kiss on her mouth. "You were young. You needed a job. He took advantage of you, Holly, of an opportune moment."

She waved away his merciful opinion as he returned to the freezer. She'd learned a lot about herself since this mess began, and she'd learned a lot about her ex as well. "He doesn't understand the meaning of the word 'compromise.'"

Evan took an ice cream from the freezer and shrugged dramatically. "Well, if that's true, you can forget negotiating for one. You're going to have to fight fire with fire. Have you considered hiring a private investigator?" He looked over his shoulder when she didn't answer.

They stared long and hard at each other. "Well, Evan, no I haven't. Somehow that seems awfully underhanded. Sleazy, you know?"

Evan continued to stare. This time he had no comment.

"You think I'm still being naive, don't you?" When he looked at his toes and still didn't answer, she continued, "Maybe I should at least consider your suggestion. Do you know any investigators?"

"I can put you in touch with someone." His elbow made contact with the freezer door, and it closed with a *thunk*. "Or I can handle it for you."

"This is going a little too fast. I'm not even sure what I'd ask a private investigator to do. Do you have to use them often in your work?"

"No." He crossed the kitchen to where she sat on the counter, unwrapped the ice cream, and handed it to her. He slid her to the edge of the counter, and opening her knees, stepped into the space between them.

She hadn't wanted this conversation in the first place, and now, by the tone of his voice and shifting interest, Evan seemed to be tiring of it too. Still, the idea of double-crossing Stu at his own game was intriguing. Resting one wrist on his shoulder, she bit off a small piece of the orange sherbet coating. "Do you look them up in the yellow pages under detectives or private investigators? No, forget I asked that. I don't think I like the idea."

He slipped his hands under her bottom and pulled her hard against him. "Let's talk about this later." He took a bite of the ice cream, then skillfully blended the orange flavor of his mouth with hers. "Much later," he said, wrapping her legs around his waist and lifting her into his arms.

While he climbed the stairs and headed down the hall to his room, thoughts of her ex-husband and private investigators vanished. Melting ice cream and orange sherbet began trickling down her wrist, but before she could halt the flow, Evan took care of it.

"That tastes great on your skin," he said with an exaggerated growl.

"Do you always have such a big appetite after you make love?"

"After?" He stopped walking to lick the sweet, sticky liquid from her fingers. "You mean before, don't you?"

"What is this thing you have for Creamsicles?" she whispered against his ear.

He walked into the bedroom. His breath was coming faster, but Holly knew it had nothing to do with carrying her up the stairs and down the hall to his room. "That's a rather personal question, Glory Girl." His tongue explored the small hollow at the base of her throat.

"Perhaps," she managed, "you . . . ahhhh . . . should explain."

"I think I'd rather show you," he said, kicking the bedroom door shut.

The air was fragrant with fresh tomatoes, peppers, and basil, and Holly inhaled it like expensive perfume. The Cape Shell garden had been overflowing with produce, and she was glad they'd thought to bring a basket of it to New York. After piercing a tomato with a long-handled fork Holly plunged it into the boiling water and waited for its thin red skin to split. The simple tasks of chopping, mincing, stirring, and tasting had taken on a new sensual dimension. She'd always enjoyed cooking, but it came to mind as she worked that preparing food for Evan was a special joy.

Gershwin's "Rhapsody in Blue" played as she glanced across Evan's sunny penthouse kitchen and through the open French doors to the terrace. Stretched out on an oversize lounge, he looked up and waved as he spoke into the portable phone. She blew him a kiss, then laughed softly to herself as she dropped fresh basil leaves into the simmering sauce. He'd likened the ambience of his penthouse to an upscale dentist's office. She looked around at the gleaming white surfaces, harlequin tile floor, and copper pots. How could he think such a thing? Nothing could have been further from the truth. They'd arrived two hours ago, and already all three thousand square feet felt cozy to her.

He came up behind her, encircling her waist and nuzzling her behind an ear. He was glad he'd given his housekeeper the week off. Privacy had become very precious.

"You may congratulate me. I've just become an uncle for the eleventh time." Still holding her, he allowed enough maneuvering space to receive an awkward kiss on his cheek.

"Congratulations."

"My brother Ken and his wife, Carla, had a little girl, Annabelle. Seven pounds, thirteen ounces, blue eyes and curly brown hair." He took the wooden spoon from Holly and placed it in the spoon rest. "Come on. I'll show you some photographs of the family."

Holly hesitated. "Wait. The noon news is about to come on. I think I'd better watch it."

"We, Holly. We'd better watch it," he admonished, shaking his finger at her. "We're in this together." He turned on the little TV set at the breakfast bar.

Five minutes later Holly turned toward him and smiled. "Dennis Cracci never mentioned me. And you know what? I don't think he's going to, not for a while anyway."

Evan gave her a skeptical look.

Her arms, which had been tightly wrapped around her waist, stretched wide apart. "Think about it. Why should he tell anyone he saw me on the Cape Shell boardwalk last night? That would be taking a chance someone else could find me. He's not about to let that happen. He could check out my apartment here in town, but he'll never think to look for me at your place."

He watched as she shut her eyes tightly and whispered a fervent, "Yes!"

It was almost more than he could bear. His Holly ecstatic over a temporary victory, when the real battle hadn't yet begun. Stu Hamilton's deadline was a couple of weeks away. "Glory Girl, I want you to think about what I said. About hiring a private investigator."

"I don't like that idea. There's something so . . . underhanded about it." She returned to the stove and stirred fresh-ground pepper into the pot of sauce. "Here,"—she lifted the spoon and, with a cupped hand safely beneath it, carefully brought the rich sauce to his lips—"taste this and tell me what you think."

He gave up with a smile, wanting, as she did, to forget the rest of the world. To live in a present filled with delicious food, a newborn niece, and most of all Holly's love and laughter . . . and that look that told him there was a heaven here on earth. Tomorrow didn't exist, but this afternoon did. And so did tonight. Evan lowered his head, dutifully tasted the sauce, then licked his lips. "Hey, that's delicious. When do we eat?"

"Just as soon as the water's ready I'll boil the fusilli." Opening a package of the corkscrew-shaped pasta, she took one out, snapped it in half, and held a piece to each of her ears. "What do you think?"

He eyed her with roguish suspicion. "Bow ties I've eaten. Angel hair too. But, that's some pretty twisted pasta you managed to slip past my doorman."

"Be kind. My mother makes this for my dad all the time, and he's as straight as they come."

Laughing, he reached to turn off the TV, when a weather map of the Caribbean appeared on the screen. He'd never passed up a look at a weather map since his first flying lesson seventeen years ago. A tropical storm spinning through the Caribbean seemed determined to turn itself into a hurricane. He watched the report a few more moments, then picked up the wall phone and dialed ASI's flight operations. Hurricane season had arrived, and even a possible hurricane had an immediate effect on flight plans.

The large clay tiles were warm beneath Holly's bare feet when they took their plates out on the terrace twenty minutes later. The day was clear and pleasantly warm. "Lucky us. It feels more like autumn than August."

Evan pulled out a chair from the glass-top table, and when she sat down he pushed aside her single braid and kissed her on the back of her neck. He gave her shoulders a gentle squeeze. "Yes, lucky us," he agreed.

She leaned her cheek on his hand, then took it in her own to kiss it. For a long, sweet moment they looked out over the city. Central Park lay before them, sumptuous in several shades of green and as richly textured as a brocaded pillow, its lake shimmering like metallic threads in the noon sun. She closed her eyes, wanting to remember everything about this moment. Every sight, every sound, every feeling.

After lunch Evan took her to his study, where the walls were covered with photographs. Some were black-and-white, others yellowed with age, and the more recent ones were in color. The subject matter varied, but Holly could see that all involved moments memorable for happiness. In one, Evan and his childhood friends crowded the end of the bay dock, all holding up crabs they'd caught; in another, dressed in lifeguard uniforms, a teenage Evan and his brothers and friends formed a human pyramid on the beach. One yellowed newspaper-clipped photo featured Evan and a pretty girl tossing pizza dough at the Cape Shell Café. Several featured Evan's parents cuddling healthy, energetic grandchildren. As she looked at each photo, Evan gave a running commentary on all the parties involved.

"How many brothers do you have?"

"There are five of us." He pointed to one of the larger photos picturing at least twenty different smiling people in front of a pistachio-colored lawn tent with a rather substantial-looking house in the background. Among the many smiling faces was Evan holding a little boy on his shoulders. The child appeared to be mashing cake into Evan's ear.

Holly leaned closer and tapped her fingernail on the glass covering it. "Tell me about this one."

"My dad's official family retirement party, right before they moved down to Naples, Florida. We all surprised him with it up at the Saddle River house. I'm holding Nathan, my brother Rick's son. It took me an hour to work all that cake out of my ear."

Holly watched his animated expression as he explained. "Nathan was having the time of his life up there on my shoulders. Jayne, she's over here, next to Ken," he said pointing to a pouting child, "was mad as a baby hornet. She doesn't like to share her Uncle Evan's shoulders with anyone."

She sat on the end of his desk and smiled at him. "You enjoy your family a lot, don't you? Especially the children."

He nodded. "You'll get to meet them one of these days. We all try to get together at my folks' place down in Naples for Thanksgiving or Christmas. It's a three- or four-day circus, only the food and facilities are a lot nicer."

Holly noticed the little girl wasn't the only pouting face in the photo. An overly thin blonde stood off to the right with her arms crossed in front. She was staring at Evan. Holly asked the silent question with her eyes, knowing intuitively who the woman must be.

"Cynthia, my ex-wife."

"You're so good with children. Can I ask why you didn't have any with her?"

His laugh was sharp and short. "It wasn't from

my lack of pleading with her. She kept saying she wasn't ready, or the time wasn't right. The fact is, she got so wrapped up in her parties and trips that she didn't want to rearrange her life for a baby. I'll never forget the time Annie kind of thrust Peter into Cynthia's arms. The kid stiffened out, screamed, and wet all over her. All I heard on the way home was how her silk dress was ruined."

Holly couldn't help it. Laughing, she reached out for his hands. "Evan, Annie told me about that."

"What she didn't tell you, and what no one knows, is that a few weeks after that Cynthia had a miscarriage."

Holly felt the smile draining from her face. "I'm sorry, Evan. They say miscarriages just happen sometimes. Maybe—"

"Holly, I didn't know she'd been pregnant until she had the miscarriage. She was almost three months along when it happened. I asked when she was going to tell me, but she wouldn't look at me. Then I asked if she'd planned on going through with the pregnancy. She said, 'You'll never know, will you?' That finished it. Things went from bad to worse between us. I knew we didn't have a chance, and we divorced shortly after that."

She stared at him for a long moment. He'd been dragged through an emotional wringer by a manipulative spouse, just like she had been. That he had been so honest about it had given her a painful pleasure in the deepest part of her heart. She felt an overwhelming need to tell him the specifics of her own betrayal.

Dropping his hands, she stepped back and

leaned against the desk. "Last week we had a lot of time to talk. I told you some things about my marriage and about Stu, but I didn't tell you everything. I'd made it clear to him right from the beginning that I wouldn't be interested in modeling forever. That eventually I'd want children, a house, a couple of dogs—a normal life." She opened her hands, palms up. "The time came when I'd had enough of modeling, and I told him so. When I said I wanted to have a child, he tried to talk me out of it. When I wouldn't back down, he told me he'd had a vasectomy and that I could forget having children. The cruelest part was that he'd had the vasectomy years ago and never mentioned it until he had to." She made fists with her hands and slammed them to her thighs. "Why are people so selfish, so self-centered? Whatever happened to being honest with one another, Evan? With listening, with sharing? With talking things out?"

He pulled her into his arms and stroked her cheek with the backs of his fingers. "You don't have to think about those things anymore, Holly. It's going to be different from now on." He slanted his mouth over hers, kissing her gently. "Trust me, darling. It's going to be very, very different."

"I know that now," she whispered, pulling his head back to hers.

Early that evening Evan took a phone call from ASI and ended up going in to his office. When he returned, he found Holly on the terrace. The familiar setting suddenly wasn't so familiar anymore. He once thought the miniature lights spiraling around the ball-shaped shrubs and tiny leafy trees gave the terrace an oddly whimsical look, but now he saw it all as magical because Holly was there. As he approached her he slipped out of his jacket and loosened his tie.

Her tight ivory off-the-shoulder top accentuated the width of her shoulders and her sculpted waist. The short suede skirt hugging her hips was hot-pepper red, and when she leaned against the rail, it shifted higher. Evan smiled. Her leggy, satiny-skin perfection was only enhanced by the fact that she was barefoot.

He went to stand at the rail, several feet away from her. When she turned to acknowledge him, he kept his distance, enjoying her beauty, her loving look, and the anticipation of her touch. "I'm home," he said, appreciating the way her skin glowed in the moonlight.

"I'm glad." A flirting breeze continued teasing the ends of her hair. She smiled, obviously enjoying the anticipation building between them. Her smile continued to challenge him until he couldn't stand not touching her. "Get over here," he said, before surrendering with laughter.

She went at once into his outstretched arms.

He growled into her hair. "I missed you."

"I missed you more." She trailed kisses along his jaw.

"Impossible."

He picked her up and settled her, laughing, onto the oversize lounge behind the trellis. When he moved up beside her, he pulled her back into his arms. "I want to know everything you did while I was gone."

She lay against him in the crook of his arm, the top of her head inches from his lips. "Everything?

Like, I painted my toenails?" She playfully lifted one foot. "See? Now they match my skirt."

"Ooooh, I love this skirt," he said, pretending a great and serious interest in the material. He ran his hand down her hip, making her laugh while he examined the stitching and how the hem was turned.

"So do I," she said, bringing his hand to her mouth. "Suede's so sensuous."

He traced her lips with his fingers. She sucked one into her mouth, then slowly took it out. His world had suddenly narrowed to her mouth and eyes and the tightening sensation within.

"What else did you do while I was gone?"

"I really did miss you, Ev." Her tone sounded something like an embarrassed apology.

Intrigued, he asked, "And?"

"I hope you don't mind, but I put on a little of your after-shave."

Her confession of such an intimate act thrilled him. "Where did you put it on?"

"In your bathroom."

He swallowed. "I mean where did you put it on your body?"

She touched the swell of her breasts. "Here." Her voice was becoming throaty and slow. "But it doesn't smell the way I imagined it would."

He took an extra breath before he spoke. "Well, uh, how did you imagine it?"

"Like, it would be having you near."

"And it's not?"

She shook her head. "The scent mixed with me and it was a little like having us . . . together." She rubbed his cheekbone with her thumb. "Only,

Evan, there's nothing quite like us together."
Touching her lips to his, she fed him tiny kisses.

"Lord, Holly. You're killing me." He took her in
his arms and turned her onto her back. As the
stars came out, they made love, enthralling each
other with the depths of their passion. They awoke
in the early morning sunlight still entwined within
the cocoon of a cotton throw, reluctant to move
and lose their closeness. She drew light, lazy
circles on his chest with her fingernail.

"Holly?"

"Hmmm?"

"I have to go back into the office this morning. I
wish I didn't have to, but I do."

Lifting up on her elbows, she gave him a smack-
ing kiss. "I wish you could call me, but I don't
want to answer the phone in case someone recog-
nizes my voice."

"Just let it ring until the answering machine
clicks on. When you hear my voice you can turn it
off, and we can talk."

She snuggled against him once more. "Do you
have to go real soon?"

He reached under the cotton throw. "Not real
soon," he said pulling her to him.

An hour after he'd left the apartment the phone
rang. Holly had been cleaning up the lunch dishes
and, dropping a pot into the sink, made a dash for
the living-room phone on the first ring. On the
third ring she was lying stomach down on the
leather sofa, and on the fourth ring her hand
hovered over the receiver. The answering machine
clicked on, Evan's recorded greeting played

through, and a masculine voice with a thick Brooklyn accent filled the room.

"Mr. Jamieson? Hackford of Hackford Investigative Agency here. I was out on a case last night and didn't get your message until this morning. No need to give up, Mr. Jamieson. This shouldn't take much longer."

Holly pushed herself up from the sofa as she continued listening. Evan had mentioned that he used detectives occasionally. What a coincidence that one should be calling. She started back to the kitchen.

The voice on the phone continued. "Some of the preliminaries you, I am sure, already know. The ex-husband does good work, but hasn't been putting much out in the last year. The wife, on the other hand, has quit modeling altogether."

Holly grabbed the doorjamb between the kitchen and living room. Modeling? Her heart began pounding in her chest. Had the man said modeling?

"I'll have the reports on the Hamiltons over to you soon, Mr. Jamieson." A few seconds of silence were broken only by the rustle of paper on the other end. "She's got a nice tush," Mr. Hackford offered, before hanging up.

Holly felt the blood draining from her face and her insides turning to jelly.

"Why did you do it?" she whispered fiercely. "Why?"

She pressed her back against the doorjamb and slid slowly to the floor. He'd lied when he said they were going to find a solution to this problem together. Knowing she didn't want to use a detective, he'd betrayed her by going behind her back and hiring one anyway. And for what? She laughed bitterly. Business. First and foremost, to insure his business interests.

And having Stu investigated wasn't the worst part, Evan was having her investigated as well. Investigated like a common criminal.

What else did he want to know about her? And why hadn't he asked her? Why hadn't he trusted her? She shook her head. There had to be some understandable and acceptable reason for what he'd done. She went over it one more time, hoping against hope she could find one. With the machine beeping in the background, she finally gave in. There was no good reason, and the facts couldn't be denied. Even though she'd taken her time trusting him, in the end he hadn't deserved that trust.

Shoving back her hair, Holly rose to her feet. Her initial shock was turning to anger. She went to the answering machine and slammed her hand on the erase button. Although it would take him a while to figure out why, Evan's summer project had just ended.

"Holly? Come on in here, I've got a surprise for you."

Evan dropped his briefcase to the floor, then carefully set the box next to it. Two West Highland white terrier puppies with perky red bows scrambled to escape. He tipped the box gently, allowing them to tumble onto the red-and-white Oriental rug.

"Holly?"

Where was she? He pushed the kitchen door open, and the two puppies scampered between his legs. He pulled a bowl from a cupboard, filled it with water, and, calling her name again, set it down. The two terriers inspected the bowl, then made their way straight to the French doors and out onto the terrace. Maybe she was there; that's where he'd found her last time he'd returned.

She wasn't there. His pace quickened as he searched the apartment. She wasn't anywhere. And her clothes were gone. He walked back into the living room and sank slowly into one of the tan leather sofas. He took a short, nervous breath. He'd finally got her to trust him, so the thought that she might have left him was absurd. Wasn't it? An anxious feeling began working its way into his chest. What could have happened to make her vanish like this? Leaning forward, he rubbed his face until it stung. Dammit! There were so many things they had yet to do with their lives.

He stood up, pulled a small velvet box from his pocket, and lifted the top. Nestled in the white satin was a fantasy-fashioned citrine ring. He'd never seen another ring like it. The fiery light reflecting from the orange wedge-cut stone, flanked by two diamonds, seemed to sing out to him from the store window. He knew it was meant for her, and he knew he was meant to give it to her. He closed the box and slipped it back into his pocket.

The two puppies with matching red bows had come in from the terrace and were sitting at his feet, looking up at him. He lowered himself onto his haunches and scratched their ears. "It's not over yet, guys."

Eight

When a wave of nausea hit again, Holly fanned herself with the budget report and waited for it to pass. Breathing deeply and slowly, she looked around her Lemon Aid office, steadfastly holding on to the victory of simply being there. For the past three weeks she'd been able to slip into Lemon Aid's Manhattan offices undetected by the press. Of course, the addition of a short brown wig, baggy beige clothes, and unfashionable glasses had helped. But, three weeks . . .

Three weeks without him.

There hadn't been an hour that she hadn't thought about him. Hadn't longed for his teasing. His tender touch. The deep rumble in his chest when he laughed. Or when he whispered. She whacked her hand on the desk. Was she *crazy*? He'd treated her like a common criminal.

Pushing up from the desk, Holly turned to the tiny window behind it. An anxious feeling coupled with fatigue was taking over where nausea left off.

She pressed her forehead against the glass. It was ridding herself of Stu that was stressing her to this point. Trying to find Stu the perfect replacement for the Glory Girl, she'd continued sending him models from every agency she could think of. Sooner or later he'd see a new face with the right bone structure and eye color. Then he'd forget he ever thought he needed her. It was going to work. It had to work.

Twisting the budget report into a tight cylinder, she squeezed it in both hands, stared up at the ceiling, and sighed. Why she should be adding to her stress by feeling guilty about leaving Evan was beyond her comprehension. Though her memories of their time together brought back strong emotions, she reminded herself how unspeakably he'd ended up treating her. In fact, if she saw him right now, she'd tell him a thing or two.

The door behind her opened.

"Holly?"

She whirled around. "Oh, it's you, Dave."

Dave squeezed into the tiny office. "Did I scare you? You look a little pale."

"No. It gets a little close in here with the door shut."

"Are you sure that's the reason?"

"Maybe I'm coming down with something. I got sick on chicken broth yesterday, and I feel queasy today."

Dave looked decidedly uncomfortable. "You're, uh, certain you couldn't be . . . Holly, when my wife was . . ." He took another half step toward her and leaned over her desk. "Have you been sick in the morning?"

"Not funny, Dave. If this feeling has a name, it's stress."

He stared at her a moment longer, then shrugged. "Well, I can relate to that. Waiting around to see where a hurricane's going to hit isn't a laughing matter."

Laughter. She hadn't laughed since the last time she was with Evan. "Then there's been no update about where Hurricane Celise will hit?"

He shook his head.

"So what can I do for you?"

He hesitated. "Maybe it's what I can do for you."

"What's going on?" She tossed the budget report on the desk and pointed to the central suite of offices beyond her own postage stamp–size room. "What are they saying? Or, more important, what is Mr. Willoughby saying?"

Looking behind him, Dave quickly closed the door. "He's not faulting you for your work. It's this disguise you're using to get into the office."

Holly scratched the side of her head where the short brown wig was itching her again. "What difference does it make if I'm wearing a wig?"

"It's your, uh, low profile. Mr. Willoughby says he wants to know how you can expect to be spokesperson for Lemon Aid when you haven't been seen in public for weeks. When you hide in here every time a visitor or a reporter shows up. He keeps observing that you could've had a bigger office, but you chose this broom closet instead." Dave cleared his throat and stared at the curled budget report on her desk. "Someone said maybe we should consider a sports figure for spokesperson."

The tension was beginning to build across her

forehead. She'd been hearing the whispers and noticing a gradual change of attitude among the Lemon Aid workers. They were polite but stand-offish. Holly sat down and, resting an elbow on the desk, rubbed her brow. "What else?"

"Holly, those rumors about a second poster are getting stronger every day. Dennis Cracci brought it up on his show again last night. People around here are beginning to wonder if they're true. You've got to put those rumors to rest, or I'm afraid Willoughby's brother-in-law will end up on the board instead of you."

Holly nodded. He was right. "Thanks, Dave."

"I thought you ought to know so . . . well, so you could do something." He reached for the doorknob, but instead of twisting it he turned once again to face her. "Holly, I don't want to see Willoughby's brother-in-law get the seat. He may know how to wear a tuxedo and drink martinis at a fund-raiser, but you're the one who called the president of that pharmaceutical company and got him to donate the vitamin A when we needed it for that project in India. By the way, we'd been sending him request letters for months. How did you get him to do that?"

Holly tilted her head in a thoughtful pose. She spoke slowly. "We really needed that vitamin A, and I decided since gentle measures weren't working, I had to take a more aggressive approach. The situation those needy children were in wasn't getting any better, and actually, it was getting worse. . . . I mean, what did I have to lose?" Pushing up from her desk, she felt a tiny smile growing on her lips. "Yes, what did I have to lose?" she repeated.

Dave smoothed the back of his shoulder-length hair and laughed. "You took the bull by the horns. Well, let me know if I can help you out."

Holly reached up and tugged off the wig. "Thanks, Dave." She pitched the wig into the trash can and shook her hair free. "You already have." Picking up her purse, she followed him out. "I have to go out for a while, but I ought to be back before we close up."

When Stuart Hamilton opened the door to his studio that afternoon, he had several things to say to the person on the other side.

"Holly, you look like crap. You've gained at least five pounds, and it's all in your face. And I see you were out in the sun without sunblock. I wonder how long it'll take until those freckles disappear and your skin is back in shape. Your nose peeled, didn't it? Never mind, I don't want to know. Come on in."

She breezed by him, then turned to face him after he'd closed the door. "I'm fine, Stuart, thanks for asking. And how are you?"

"Sorry." His expression was contrite, but he still looked unhappy about her freckled face and few extra pounds. "But now that you've stopped playing hide-and-seek and have decided you're coming back to work, someone has to tell you the truth. And why are you wearing beige? *Not* your color."

She marveled at his single-mindedness. His arrogant assumption that she was coming back to work for him took her breath away. While he circled her, studying her from different angles, she glanced around the studio. Her photos still dominated Stu's "trophy wall."

"It's time to end this, Stu."

"Whatever," he mumbled as he lifted a lock of her hair. "We're talking major split ends."

She slapped his hand away.

"Holly, there's something different about you." He rubbed his lips with his fingertips. "Definitely different. I'm wondering how I'm going to make it work for the cover of *Velvet and Lace*'s holiday issue. I've been thinking of green velvet, but somehow I don't think that's the best color. Maybe midnight blue or burgundy—"

"Did I say I was coming back to work for you?"

His eyes connected with hers. "Playing games, are we?"

"No games, Stu. No more games. I'm calling your bluff. If I don't leave here with all the photos and negatives from that Morning Glory shoot, I'm calling a press conference."

"Really. Should I be scared?"

Holly nodded. "Yes, Stu, that's exactly what you should be, because I intend to tell them what an insecure jackass you really are. I'll point out to them that your obsession with me has crippled your business. I'll tell them how you took the pictures without my permission and how you've been blackmailing me. And if you think for one minute that any model will ever trust you with a shoot, that any agency will ever waste its time sending someone to the likes of you, that any business will come to you with a project, then you're crazier than I thought. You'll spend the rest of your career photographing mousetraps and truck tires."

The animation drained from his face, leaving his mouth slack, his eyes wide, and his body frozen. "Are you serious?"

She walked forward and tapped him on the chest with her finger. "You want to take the chance to find out?"

He shook his head, forcing a shaky laugh. "You wouldn't."

"And why wouldn't I? I have nothing to lose, Stu. Nothing except your shadow." She opened her hand. "Hand them over."

He hesitated. "Hey, isn't there some way we could work this out?"

She continued, heedless of his last desperate stand. "My lawyer will be sending some papers to your lawyer. They'll say you swear you've given me all the photos and negatives and that you won't market anything with my likeness on it ever again. I know you've bet it all on me coming back, so I suggest you sign those papers quickly. That way you might have a chance to salvage your career. You've already wasted enough time turning away those models I've been sending you."

In the middle of her speech, he'd walked backward to a file cabinet behind his desk and began removing a large manila envelope. He looked up with that wide-eyed look again. "You're the one who's been sending them over here on those fake go sees?"

She nodded as she joined him by the cabinet. "All forty-two of them, Stu." She pointed to the envelope in his hands. "Is this all of it?"

"All of it," he replied.

She reached for the envelope but had to tug it

out of his hands. "Unbelievable," she whispered to herself as she made her way to the door.

"Holly?"

"What is it?"

"No hard feelings, okay?"

"The only thing I feel for you is pity."

During the taxi ride back to Lemon Aid, she examined the contents of the envelope. The negative in question was definitely more revealing than the first poster. Shot from her hips up, she was facing the camera with her arms crossed over her breasts. She held the negative to the window, studying it with a practiced eye. Not bad enough for a biker bar, but certainly not something she'd want associated with Lemon Aid. She breathed a sigh of relief as she slipped everything back into the envelope and pressed it to her breast. As soon as she got back to Lemon Aid, she was going to first shred the contents of the envelope, then burn the scraps.

By the time she'd exited the elevator, she was singing the Morning Glory Soap jingle. Mr. Willoughby and Dave, with their shirtsleeves rolled up, were deep in conversation when she arrived in the reception area. They both managed a perfunctory wave as she greeted them. She was smiling so hard her cheeks hurt.

"Mr. Willoughby. Dave. There isn't going to be a second Glory Girl poster." She reached out to take Mr. Willoughby's hand. "I'm not going to pretend I wasn't aware of your concerns. But you don't have to worry anymore." She shook the envelope. "I took care of the problem, once and for all."

Dave kissed her soundly on the cheek. "Way to go!"

A more reserved Willoughby glanced at the envelope, then back at her. He cleared his throat and nodded curtly. "Good," he allowed, then appeared to dismiss the subject as if it never happened. "We have more important matters to concern ourselves with, Holly. Hurricane Celise is hitting the island of Saint Julian as we speak. It looks as if the next few days around here are going to drain our resources and tax the real workers of this organization."

Suddenly thrust open, the door to Air Service International's conference room banged back against the wall. Evan shot to his feet to look across his conference table and over the heads of his staff. He was speechless at what he saw.

Her hair was a tousle of curls escaping from an off-center ponytail, her eyes were red, and she looked as if she could use a good night's sleep. Her simple white T-shirt and wide-legged indigo shorts could have suggested a harried camp counselor. They didn't. Her strained features and keen stare indicated a much deeper degree of stress.

Clutching a folder to her side, Holly dropped a canvas overnight bag on the floor, hooked an enormous pair of sunglasses over her waistband, and walked boldly toward the table. Her foot caught on the aluminum leg of a tripod, tipping it and the map it held to the floor. Heedless of the two staff members scrambling to right the mess, she continued looking at Evan. Only at Evan.

"You said if I ever needed you, you'd be there for

me. Well, I need you now." She studied him anxiously. In his crisp white shirt, red silk tie, and charcoal trousers he looked like what he was, the consummate corporate executive. With his suit jacket draped over the back of his chair and his shirtsleeves rolled halfway up his forearms, he looked, too, like the down-to-earth, accessible problem solver she knew him to be. Seconds passed crystallizing into a heavy silence. When Evan didn't respond, she continued in a whisper, "Please, Evan, I really need you."

"Mr. Jamieson, I'm sorry, but she refused to wait. I'll call security if you think it's necessary." Tally, armed with a handful of sharp pencils, had followed Holly in and was keeping both eyes on her. So were all of the men and women at the table.

Evan waved his hand toward the door. "Out. Everyone out of here."

There was a second of hesitation, then chairs were pushed back and people gathered up their papers and started shoving them into their brief-cases.

"Who is she?"

"I thought her hair was a darker red. . . ."

"I didn't think he was seeing anyone."

"My son has this poster. . . ."

Whispers filled the room like a swirling haze, but his burning stare cut through it all to Holly. When the last of the staff had filed from the room and the door was finally shut, he closed his eyes and exhaled.

"Are you all right?" he asked evenly, his finger-tips poised on the table in front of him.

"Me? Yes, I'm fine."

Again, quietly. "Are you being followed?"

She shook her head. "It's not that, it's—"

He lifted his head, his gaze connecting with hers instantly. "I called Annie. I searched everywhere in Cape Shell. I've bribed your doorman here in New York, and each night I've been glued to the TV in case Dennis Cracci knows something I don't. Hell, I even phoned your parents in Arizona."

"I know. I called them too. They said you were very nice—"

"Where have you been for the last three weeks?"

"Down in the Village. I've been staying with one of the office workers from Lemon Aid. I'm sorry if I caused you any worry, but—"

"Caused me any worry? I've been out of my mind with it!" He was making his way along the chairs and down the length of the table. "We've got some talking to do. I want to know what you were thinking when you left like that? Why didn't you ask me about—"

He was a few feet away from her when she threw up one hand and stepped backward. "Stop. I didn't come about us."

Evan stopped. He braced one hand on the back of a chair and ran the other across his forehead. "You try a man's patience, Glory Girl."

"Evan, just listen. Hurricane Celise hit the leeward islands in the Caribbean last night, and things are terrible down there. One of the worst hit was the island of Saint Julian."

Evan pointed to a map of the Caribbean now leaning against the wall. "I'm well aware of it. We were having an emergency meeting for our charter division when you dropped in. With most scheduled airline service suspended in that area, we've been flooded with requests for charter planes. Property owners want to see the damage—"

Holly was clutching a folder of papers and nodding furiously. "Yes," she cut in. "That's why I'm here. I need to get down there, down to Saint Julian as quickly as possible."

"You own land on Saint Julian?"

"No. It's for Lemon Aid. It's a chance for me to do something worthwhile." She shook her head; she wasn't explaining it right. "I have to do this. And I can do it if you . . ." She stopped, forcing herself to look away from him. It wasn't easy. His eyes were communicating a thousand things, and she didn't want to know any of them.

"I've missed you, Glory Girl."

A stillness settled over the room, locking them into the echo of his words. Her love, her lost hope, her raw need, pulsed through her like a hot braid of pleasure and pain. Holly lowered her eyelids, then her head. She was afraid of this. Afraid that he'd lay open her heart, afraid that in doing so he'd make her bleed for him all over again. She swallowed and licked nervously at the corner of her mouth. If only she'd never loved him. If only he hadn't hurt her.

"I'm not here about us. It's about Lemon Aid. . . ."

"Dammit, Holly. Is this about you getting a seat on their board?"

"No." She pushed aside a chair and stepped toward him, not daring to touch him. "I don't care about the board. It's about babies. Newborn babies that aren't going to have a chance if medical supplies aren't delivered soon. Evan, there's a maternity hospital, a center for high-risk pregnancies, in that area. The hospital's been damaged, and most of its equipment destroyed. I've managed to get replacement incubators and two generators to run them, but I can't get a flight down there to get them delivered."

He rubbed the side of his mouth as he stared at her. After everything, this. Whatever it was that had separated them, she'd put it aside and had come to him for help. He shook his head in amazement.

She dropped the folder onto the desk. "What do you want me to say? I'm sorry? I'm sorry, then. I—I messed up." She turned away from him, and sank down into a chair. "If you could have heard that radio transmission from the island this morning. They sounded so desperate." She rubbed at her knees. "They have so little, and we have so much." Her voice choked with emotion. "I don't know where else to go." Tears streamed down her face, making dark spots on her shorts. She didn't bother trying to stem the flow.

Evan did. He pulled a handkerchief from his pocket and knelt down in front of her. After he dabbed away her tears, he lifted her chin. "I don't know why you couldn't have waited to talk to me, Holly. And right now, I don't care. I'm just so damn glad to see you." He pressed his fingers to the sides of her face, making her look at him. "Of course I'll take you to Saint Julian. You know I could never say no to you."

Her carefully constructed wall crumbled, releasing her from her resolve. Holly's arms went around him. She held on to him like a rock in a stormy sea, drawing strength from his embrace, and solace from the caress of his hands. Her body heaved with each sob, while her tears soaked the shoulder of Evan's shirt. She tried not to think about the guilty pleasure of having him so near, about this stolen, tender moment that shouldn't be. But it was no use.

After a while Evan stroked her hair. "Shhhh. It's okay. It's going to be fine." When he heard her hiccup, he pulled back just enough to look at her. He handed her the handkerchief, and she took it and blew her nose. "Did you know you get all puffy when you cry?" he said teasingly.

Tilting her head, she managed a sniffle and a nod.

"And that your nose is all red?"

She shrugged and gave a convulsive little laugh.

"Holly, I'll always be here for you. You should never, ever doubt that."

She nodded once more, noting the huskiness in his voice. She fought to remember why loving him was wrong. How could enjoying him for a few minutes make things worse? How could it all have turned out so wrong? She thought back to the moments they'd shared. The fun, the passion, the tender care he'd taken with her, and the pure joy of all of it. The shared delight in things simple, from Creamsicles to little Paula's laughter—Paula and Peter and his new niece Annabelle. That night on the boardwalk and afterward on the beach. Her breath caught in her throat. If only he'd been satisfied with her explanations, if only he'd trusted her. Her chin trembled. If only, in spite of it all, he could have loved her. She closed her eyes; at least he'd never said it.

He whispered it. "I love you, Holly."

Her eyes widened as she lowered the handkerchief to her lap. She dropped her head onto his shoulders and cried for a full five minutes.

Holly followed Evan out of the conference room and into a fully packed reception area. It appeared no one who'd attended the emergency charter division meeting had returned to his or her office. Hanging back, Holly watched Evan retake control of the group.

He checked the notes in the folder Holly had brought him. "Jake, I'm going to need about a hundred fifty cubic feet of cargo space. We'll be carrying five hundred pounds of equipment, so get down to flight maintenance and have them remove enough seats from Two Fifty Seven Juliet Sierra."

"But that Falcon belongs to—"

"Just do it, Jake."

"Where to, Mr. Jamieson?" asked one of the men.

"File a flight plan to Saint Julian. The ETD is twelve hundred hours, and put these names on the manifest." He handed a paper to one of the women.

The woman looked at the names, then at Holly. Then all of them looked at Holly.

"Suzanne," he said as he looked around the

room, "we'll be using our usual discretion when it comes to the privacy of our client."

The woman looked at Evan and nodded. "Of course, sir."

"Pepper, contact the airport in Saint Julian to make sure that runway is clear of debris. Everyone speaks English down there, so there won't be any language problem." He turned to his right. "Mark, call for weather. I know there weren't any storms there two hours ago, but I don't want any surprises."

The one thing she'd never doubted was his ability to take care of business. Holly watched the dizzying energy Evan generated around him. People were scurrying toward phones, into elevators, and down hallways. A sense of calm descended over her for the first time in three weeks. He was everything she'd expected and more.

"Who's on for this flight, Mr. Jamieson?"

"Put Byron Gerardo in the right seat."

"Lead pilot?"

Evan looked up from the folder. "Me."

"You? But you have that contract to sign with Stoddard at one this afternoon. He's expecting a final walk-through on his Falcon."

He closed the folder and tucked it under his arm. "Well, he's not getting it, because I'm taking his Falcon to Saint Julian. It's the only one available that's big enough for the cargo and can take that runway."

Several of the men and women shot questioning looks at each other.

"Do we have a problem here?" asked Evan.

"No, sir," the group answered in unison.

• • •

Holly and Evan rode side by side in the back of a Jeep through the devastated island of Saint Julian. The smell of fresh-cut wood along with wet earth swirled around them. The sights kept them both from speaking for several miles. Metal roofs and broken wood siding were scattered over the lush green landscape. A small pack of dogs sniffed at the carcass of a dead cow. One man walked along the roadside carrying a framed photo in one hand and a broken platter in the other. Small groups of people looked toward the vehicles as they picked through angular cement and cinder-block shells. The devastation surrounding them continued unbroken, each sight worse than the previous. It was like a nightmare, a carnival ride through hell.

"You didn't have to come," she told him as their Jeep bounced along the rut-filled road.

"Would you have preferred I stay on the plane eating doughnuts and drinking coffee?"

"No. I didn't mean it that way. You could have left us here and gone straight back. We would have found another way home." She stared straight ahead. "I know how important your work is to you. I wouldn't want to keep you from it a minute longer than I had to."

"What the hell does that mean?"

She moved to the far side of the vehicle. "If you'd left here when you had the chance, you might have gotten that plane back before the news crews arrive and see it. It's the first relief plane down here, and it's going to be on every news show by tomorrow morning. Then you'll never be able to hide from Mr. Stoddard the fact that you flew the Glory Girl in it." She held back a wild lock of hair and waited for him to admit what she'd said was true. As soon as he had, she was going to tell him about her visit to Stu. That if he'd truly trusted her, things would be different between them today. And then, if there was anything left of her, she was going to ask him why he'd ripped her heart out by saying he loved her.

"I had no intention of hiding that fact from Stoddard or anyone. Holly, why are we talking about Stoddard when we need to talk about us? A few hours ago I told you I loved you. I held you in my arms while you cried about it. Dammit, Holly, you can't keep pretending I never said it."

Before she could answer, the Jeep lurched, then stopped behind the truck it had been following. A wave of nausea hit her, and her hand went to her mouth.

Evan touched the small of her back. "Are you all right? You're shaking."

"I'm fine." She stood up and reached to touch the driver on the shoulder. "What are we stopping for?"

"We're here," he explained, pointing over the hood of the Jeep. "This is the hospital."

She felt Evan's hand slide away.

"My God," Evan said.

Striving for distance from Evan had been her main concern, but now she reached out for him. There was no hospital, only two large tents, mounds of rubble, and an eerie stillness. Holly caught her breath and allowed Evan to help her out of the Jeep. For a long moment his steadying hands were the only life in a sea of dead calm. Then the rest of the volunteer group climbed out of the truck. Whispers of disbelief floated around them.

Suddenly two people in surgical scrubs emerged from one of the tents and hurried toward them.

"If you're the people from Lemon Aid, we need that equipment brought in and hooked up immediately," said a doctor. "The stress of this hurricane has sent a number of women into premature labor, and we need all the help you can give us."

While the doctor began directing Evan and the other volunteers in unloading the equipment, a nurse grabbed Holly's hand. Evan caught her eye and nodded reassuringly right before Holly disappeared into the tent. Inside there were half a dozen women on cots, some lying quietly, others moaning.

"I'm Francine. What's your name?"

Holly blinked several times to gather her scattered thoughts. "Holly."

"Holly, this section is our labor area." She pointed at the first cot. "And this is Maria. It's her first baby. Hold her hands. Talk to her. She's got another half hour, at least, and I've got to assist with a C-section that can't wait."

The nurse disappeared behind a curtain, and Holly stared at the woman on the cot. The woman attempted a smile, but suddenly her eyes grew large and her breathing quickened. Holly dropped to her knees and took the woman's hand.

"This is my first baby. Will you help me?"

Forcing a confident smile, Holly maneuvered onto an upturned fruit crate. "That's what I'm here for."

Around them people came and went, but Holly stayed beside Maria, swept up in the human drama. She ended up talking very little because, as her labor progressed, the pregnant woman talked incessantly. About her husband, about their unborn child, and about their modest plans to rebuild. Between the bone-crunching squeezes that accompanied each of Maria's contractions Holly listened, humbled by the simplicity of the woman's life and uplifted by her determination to not let the hurricane destroy what was left of it.

Twenty minutes after Maria was whisked away, a nurse came out from behind the curtain with a baby in her arms. Holly looked up from the stack of blankets she was folding.

"This is the nice part," said the nurse, handing the infant to Holly. "We have a bit more work to do with his mother. Just stay where you are and enjoy. This little fellow was full term and, as you can tell by his lung power, healthy."

Holly cradled the infant, quieting him and marveling at the lightness of her bundle. The compelling movements and soft sounds now emanating from the newborn in her arms tugged at her heart. Through this disaster had come a survivor. Small and precious. Real and wanted. And loved. Life was already renewing itself, expressing the truest miracle of them all. She lifted the baby to kiss him on the forehead.

Evan's smiling face caught her eyes. She saw his straight, even nose, his finely chiseled lips moist with coffee, and that one lock of hair curved over his forehead leaning over her and the baby. The quiet pleasure of the moment warmed her, and she decided to forget her personal hurt for the time being

"What have they had you doing?"

He lowered himself on his haunches and, inhaling the aroma of the coffee in his hands, smiled. "Manly things," he said.

"What manly things?"

"Assembling stuff with wrenches and screwdrivers. Hooking up cables and wires. And moving large and very heavy objects." He reached out to stroke the newborn's cheek. "Who's your new friend?"

"I don't think he has a name yet." Looking around the tent, she smiled wistfully. "You know, I thought I wanted to be a nurse once. I even convinced Annie to be a candy striper with me when we were in the eighth grade."

"Holly, when I came looking for you a little while ago, you were doing a wonderful job with that woman. Why didn't you become a nurse? What happened?"

"I got lousy grades in chemistry."

He nodded. "Too bad I didn't know you then. Chemistry was one of my best subjects. I could have tutored you."

"Imagine that. Who knows where we'd be today?"

He shrugged with comical drama.

She tilted her head. "Did you always want to be a pilot?"

"Always. Never a doubt about it."

The nurse appeared from behind a curtain. "Take a break, Holly. You deserve it," she said, taking the baby.

Holly followed Evan out of the tent and into the field of rubble. Without the distraction of the warm bundle, reality and negative feelings began returning. She took a deep breath and let it out slowly. "Staying down here like this can't be good for your business. Do you think Mr. Stoddard will cancel because you and the plane weren't there this afternoon?"

"Possibly." He lowered the cup and raised his eyebrows. "But sometimes in life we have to choose. I chose to come, and I chose to stay. And I'll take full responsibility for the consequences of those choices."

"You'll end up regretting this."

He set the cup on a makeshift table and took her by the elbows. "What's going on? What are you trying to say?"

This wasn't the time or the place to talk, and she instantly regretted her comments. She looked up at him. Too late. She'd pushed him too far, and he wasn't going to let her off the hook.

"I guess I was questioning why you were doing this, Evan. What made you drop everything and come down here?"

"Besides the fact that you asked me? Holly, you have to figure out what's important, what has to be done, and then do it."

Releasing her elbows, he studied her quietly, then appeared to come to a decision. "Come with me, I want to show you something."

They made their way through the rubble toward the tent he'd been working in. He drew her back when she would have entered.

"I'm proud to know you, Holly, and proud you came to me for help. I'll never regret coming here. In fact, I'll always be thankful you asked because this experience reminded me of something we all tend to forget."

He lifted the flap and took her inside. Lined

against the wall were three of the incubators they'd brought to Saint Julian. Each held a tiny, fragile infant. Each breathing, each moving, each someone's treasured miracle.

"We're all survivors, Holly. And no matter what disasters occur, life goes on."

Nine

"But why do I have to sign this charter-paper release thing?" she asked as he half pulled, half pushed her past his staff and down the hall to his office. "I spent last night on a cot, part of this morning on an airplane, and the last thing I want to do is push papers around your desk. Can't you send it over to Lemon Aid later on today? Can't someone else sign it?"

"Hold my calls," Evan said to Tally as he maneuvered a struggling Holly closer to his office.

"Mr. Stoddard's in the building, Mr. Jamieson. He'll be up here any time now. And there are a number of press people milling around the front reception area."

Gathering Holly firmly against him, he stopped. "I want to see Stoddard."

Holly twisted to glare up at him in regretful disapproval. "I'm sure you have lots of unfinished business to take care of, so if you'll let go of—"

He pulled her into his office, shut the door, and

pressed her against it with the length of his body. "You're damn right I have unfinished business to take care of."

"Evan Jamieson, how can I sign a paper with you all over me?"

"To hell with the paper." His nostrils flared momentarily. "Don't you have something to say to me?"

The edge to his voice startled her, but she wasn't surrendering that easily. She was going to get through this. Steeling herself against the undeniable hold he had on her, she stared at his company's logo embroidered on the pocket of his shirt. "Yes," she began in a shaky voice. "On behalf of Lemon Aid—"

His cool blue eyes narrowed, and a grim expression settled on his lips. He knew what she was going to say, and he didn't want to hear it.

"Don't, Holly."

She continued anyway, determined to get through it. "—we want to thank you for the generous donation of your airplane and your time."

"Dammit! I don't want your thanks. I want an explanation for why you left me three weeks ago." He blocked her move with his knee, then jutted his chin in challenge. "You're not leaving this office until you tell me."

Twisting and turning, she tried throwing him off. She'd never seen him like this. Angry. Hurt. Fighting for an answer. And she was fighting back. After several unfruitful attempts she exhaled loudly, and gave in to the inevitability of the situation. "Okay. Let go of me, and I'll tell you."

He didn't move.

"Don't you trust me?" she snapped.

Before she could protest, his lips were on hers in a branding kiss. If he wasn't going up in smoke, she was. Struggling to turn away, she finally broke the contact and gasped for breath. "This isn't fair, Evan. This isn't fair at all."

Still holding her hands to her sides, he gentled his kisses, stringing them over her cheek and down her neck. As he continued the tender attack, her rigid posturing began to soften. Since the start of the trip, she'd managed to avoid all but the most casual contact with him. Ignoring most of his intimate glances, sidestepping any possibility of an accidental brush against him, she was even able to fight the temptation of his patient smiles. And now, when she needed most to be apart from him, her knees were buckling. Turning her face toward him, she felt his scratchy jaw against her cheek. The masculine feel of it, along with the touch of his mouth and contact with the hard length of him rippled through her body. "This isn't fair," she repeated without conviction, right before her lips brushed his ear.

He raised his head to eye level with hers. "Like it wasn't fair when you left me?" He released her hands and backed away. "Talk."

She eyed him warily. He still had that skeptical look, but his anger was in check. Breathless and trembling, she straightened her slacks, patted down the front of her blouse, and primly folded her arms over her waist. "I was under the misconception that we could trust each other. That what we told each other was the truth, the whole truth, with nothing left out." She tilted her chin and narrowed her eyes. "That we weren't sneaking

GLORY GIRL • 171

around behind the other's back with our own agendas."

Evan shrugged. "Agendas?"

"As in business agendas." She watched him for signs of an imminent confession and possible apology. What she saw was a look of bewilderment. She raised her voice and filled it with contempt. "That night on the beach I told you everything—and then what did you do?"

Disbelief took over where anger left off. "What do you mean, what did I do? I made love to you. I peeled off your clothes and made love to you on that blanket, Glory Girl."

The invasion of those tender memories threw her off course. She walked away from him, struggling to regain control. "I'm not the Glory Girl anymore," she said with more passion than triumph.

"Your ex decided not to market the second poster?"

"That's not exactly how it happened." She pressed her palm to her chest and whirled around. "*I* decided for him. With a little creative persuasion he finally came around to accepting my decision."

Before she knew what was happening, Evan had swooped her up and was spinning around the room with her. "Outstanding! How did you manage it?"

Damning that fluttery ache in her heart, she struggled onto her feet and out of his arms. "If you'll wait a day or two, I'm sure your detective will fill you in on all the details."

"How did you find out about the detective?"

"You look a little shocked, Evan. Does it surprise you that I know you rushed out to hire him on our first morning together in New York?"

"I didn't rush right out, Holly. I'd hired that detective a long time ago."

Now she was the one in shock. "You *what*? A long time ago? You hired this guy a long time ago?" She headed for the door, but he made it there first, holding it closed.

"I had to."

"Had to?" She thumped him on the shoulder. "I thought we trusted each other, and you were having me checked out by a P.I.!"

He took her by the shoulders and, giving her a gentle shake, moved her back against the door again. "No, it was you who didn't trust me."

She stared down to where their bodies met. "But I never treated you like a criminal."

Letting go of her, his hands hovered near her body. "No," he admitted, "you never treated me like a criminal, but you didn't treat me like what I was to you, either. A friend." He backed up a step and raised a pointing finger. "Hear me out, Holly."

She nodded.

"You wouldn't tell me what was wrong, what was frightening you. Annie wouldn't tell me either. At one point, Holly, you wouldn't even walk across the patio without wearing a disguise. You hid in bushes, you answered the phone with silence, you jumped every time a hinge creaked. I started to think that someone was out to physically harm you. I couldn't ignore it. I had to do something to help you somehow. Holly, what choice did I have?"

With her hands folded in front of her, she pretended great interest in the knuckles of her thumbs. Self-doubt was already gnawing at her. She winced. "If this is true—"

"For God's sake, Holly. You're not going to tell me you don't believe me?"

Her fists balled in frustration. "Well, why didn't you tell me about hiring the guy?"

"I almost did. On Fiesta Fantasy Night, after we came back from the beach, I was feeling you out when I suggested putting a detective on Stu. You were uneasy about it, right from the beginning. Holly, our emotions were running so high that night that I wasn't thinking straight. I didn't want anything to bring us down, to bring you down, so I didn't tell you about the detective after all."

She sent him a flickering glance, then opened her hands in a gesture of helplessness. "Am I still being followed?"

"I let him go the first evening we were in New York, right before I got back to the penthouse."

Pressing her lips together to keep her embarrassed smile in check, she looked up at him. With his arms folded across his chest and his wry smile, he appeared to be daring her to prolong the situation.

"Were you ever going to tell me about it?"

He nodded once. "Yes."

The negative tension had evaporated, and a different type began developing. She stepped toward him. Dragging her fingertip along the edge of his belt, her eyes flirted with his. "Evan?"

"Hmmm?" He trailed his fingertips down the buttons of her blouse.

Shifting her body, she lifted her lips closer to his. "When were you going to tell me about it?"

He pulled her into his arms and kissed her with

a startling urgency. Glowing with a kaleidoscopic array of emotions, she matched him with an eagerness that made his blood run hot. He broke the kiss to look at her. "I was going to tell you as soon as you'd seen the puppies."

"Puppies? What puppies?"

Before he could explain, someone knocked on the door and opened it. Without letting Holly go, he looked over her shoulder.

"Mr. Stoddard. Please, come in." He felt Holly flinch, then bury her face in his shoulder.

"I see you're busy." Stoddard twisted the card-board cylinder under his arm. "Perhaps I should have waited."

"No, that's quite all right." Holly had disentagled herself from him and was trying to move away. His hand shot out to catch her and hold her.

"Jamieson, about that trip you flew to Saint Julian."

With her back to Mr. Stoddard, Holly met Evan's glance. "This was what I was afraid of all along," she said quietly. "I blew that contract for you. I'm sorry, Evan."

Evan pulled her to his side. "Yes, it was an emergency relief flight. But I'll remind you, sir, your contract had expired. The plane wasn't tech-nically yours at the time."

Stoddard waved his hand as if his inconve-nience was of no importance. "Damn fine thing you did, Jamieson. Damn fine thing. That's what I like to see. Someone who thinks quickly in an emergency. You send those contracts over to my office tomorrow and I'll sign them."

Evan reached to shake Mr. Stoddard's hand. "I thought you'd understand. Thank you, sir. It's great to have you back with ASI." He nodded toward Holly who was smiling from ear to ear. "I'd like you to meet someone."

Evan saw the man's eyes light up.

"No need for introductions, Jamieson."

As Mr. Stoddard continued staring at her, Evan spoke up. "Holly volunteers her time at Lemon Aid, and was instrumental in organizing the relief flight to Saint Julian."

Stoddard bounced a look off Evan, then refocused his attention on Holly. "I know. My people told me this morning. Uh, Miss Hamilton, could I ask a favor?"

Looking with uncertainty at Evan, she was rewarded with a smile and a nod.

"Yes, Mr. Stoddard?"

"It's for my son." He pried the thick plastic lid from the end of the cylinder and carefully slid out the contents. Holding it by two corners, he let the poster unroll in front of him. "Could you autograph this for him?"

Holly clapped her hands in delight. "I'd love to, Mr. Stoddard." After helping him smooth the poster across the desk, Evan handed her a pen. "What's your son's name?"

Stoddard looked at Evan and winked. "Well, if you'll just sign it to L.B."

While Holly signed the poster, Tally slipped into the room and whispered something in Evan's ear.

"There you go, Mr. Stoddard. Be sure to tell your son this is the only authentically signed Glory Girl poster in existence." After helping him reroll the poster and slip it back into the cylinder, she shook his hand and accepted a kiss on the cheek.

"Hope to see those contracts on my desk tomorrow, Jamieson." Patting the cylinder, he gave Evan another exaggerated wink and left.

Evan had a secret smile on his face as he took Holly into his arms. "I have a feeling if his son wants to see that poster, he'll have to ask his father for a peek."

"Why do you say that?"

"Because, Glory Girl," Evan said before kissing her on the forehead, "you signed that to L.B., and I happen to know his kid's name is Charles."

When she stopped laughing, he lifted her chin on his crooked finger. "Tally's just told me a bunch of reporters are waiting to see you in the outer office. I'll get rid of them if you want me to." His voice softened as he caressed her face. "I'll do anything you want."

"I know you would, but I don't want you to do anything. All summer long I've been taking the coward's way out. But like you said, we all have to figure out what's important, what has to be done, and then do it. It's important that I face them so I can begin to demystify the Glory Girl and get on with being me." She traced his lips with her fingertips. "It's time to stop running, don't you think?"

He nodded, then went to the door and opened it.

"Hey, there she is," a reporter shouted.

Cameras and microphones were blossoming forth as they walked into the office. As the reporters jockeyed for position around Evan and Holly, they all began shouting questions at once.

"Are you sure you want to give all this up?" Evan asked as he pointed to the frantic actions of the reporters.

"She's not about to."

Holly turned to look at the person who'd spoken. "Mr. Willoughby. What are you doing here?"

He reached for one of the microphones and, looking out at the reporters, answered her. "Ladies and gentlemen, I'm here to announce that, because of her outstanding efforts and accomplishments during the Hurricane Celise crisis, Holly Hamilton has been unanimously elected to the board of Lemon Aid. During a special meeting held this morning, she was also named official spokesperson for this fine organization." He turned to her with a look of genuine admiration. "Holly, no one deserves this honor more than you. Congratulations." He handed her the microphone and, with a kindly tone, said, "Now that you're spokesperson, perhaps you'd like to say a few words."

"Thank you, Mr. Willoughby." She looked out at the reporters. "I do want to say a few things." She waited for the group to quiet down. "There will never be another experience for me like the one I had on Saint Julian. Undoubtedly there will be other natural disasters that Lemon Aid will attend to, but this one afforded me, afforded us all, a unique opportunity." She looked at Mr. Willoughby and then at Evan. "All of us who helped on this project dug down deep within ourselves, and gave from our hearts. We've come away better for it, enriched immeasurably by what we provided to those in need and by what we shared with each other."

The ensuing silence was broken by the bell of an arriving elevator.

Dennis Cracci bounded through the separating doors, dragging his cameraman with him.

"Holly Hamilton and Evan Jamieson together

again. Or maybe I should say, together still."
Dennis attempted wriggling his way through the
group. No one budged. "Is there anything you'd
like to tell the viewers of Entertainment-4-You?"

Evan whispered in Holly's ear until a throaty
giggle escaped her.

"I would." He motioned for the reporters to move
aside and, taking Holly by the hand, walked
through the group and around Dennis Cracci. "If
you could back up a little," Evan said, motioning
with his free arm. As the group inched backward,
he reached behind him and pushed the elevator
button. Through the growing murmurs from the
group, a soft ding could be heard. The elevator
doors parted. "Back a little more." When the
reporters and cameramen had their backs against
the wall opposite the elevators, Evan nodded.
"That's good." He turned to Holly. "Ready?"

"Ready."

Hand in hand, they made a dash into the empty
car. Laughing, Holly hit the close button, and a
second later Evan pulled her into his embrace.

Dennis Cracci waved his hands as the crowd
surged toward the closing doors. "Wait! What were
you going to say?"

"Eat your heart out, America. The Glory Girl is
mine," Evan answered, just before he kissed her.

The doors closed, and a second later the elevator began its descent. He quickly hit the emergency stop button, and the elevator jolted to a stop
between floors. "I thought those people would
never leave." He smiled as Holly slid her hand over
her stomach. The craziest little smile appeared on
her face.

"Evan, I have to tell you something."

"It'll have to wait. I have to ask you something first." He reached into his pocket, pulled out a small velvet box, and opened it. He paused for a moment, and when he spoke again his voice was softer than she'd ever heard it. "The first moment I saw this I thought of you. You're one of a kind, Glory Girl."

Holly stared at the gold ring pillowed in white satin. Flanked on either side with two diamonds, the wedge of orange citrine seemed to pulsate with inner fire. He took it from the box and held it up for her closer inspection. It was the loveliest ring she'd ever seen.

"You're proposing right here in the elevator?"

He nodded. "That's right, darling. One day when our kids ask us where it happened, we'll tell them the truth—somewhere between heaven and earth. Holly, will you marry me?"

"Yes," she said, wiping away a tear before he slipped the ring on her finger. The rest of the world disappeared for a moment, leaving only a look, a touch, and one perfect kiss.

"There's just one more thing I need to know." He took a thick red-gold lock of hair and placed it behind her shoulder.

Her lips parted in surprise. "But Evan, I've told you everything." She slipped her ringed hand across her stomach. The last, most precious, secret she would share with him later tonight.

He began unbuttoning her blouse. "Not everything, Glory Girl." Sliding his thumb inside the neckline of the saffron silk, he slowly peeled away one side. "She loves me," he said before he kissed the creamy curve of her shoulder. He peeled the silk from her other shoulder, then trailed a kiss across the tops of her breasts. "She loves me not," he whispered.

Holly slipped off the blouse and allowed it to float to the carpet. "I've loved you for so long, Evan, and I'm not afraid to say it anymore. I love you." Looking up into his loving gaze, she returned to the circle of his arms. "The past is finally behind us."

"That's true," he said as he lowered her to the floor. "But you'll always be my Glory Girl."

THE EDITOR'S CORNER

Next month LOVESWEPT brings you spirited heroines and to-die-for heroes in stories that explore romance in all its forms—sensuous, sweet, heartwarming, and funny. And the title of each novel is so deliciously compelling, you won't know which one to read first.

There's no better way to describe Gavin Magadan than as a **LEAN MEAN LOVING MACHINE**, LOVESWEPT #546, by Sandra Chastain, for in his boots and tight jeans he is one dangerously handsome hunk. And Stacy Lanham has made a bet to vamp him! How can she play the seducer when she's much better at replacing spark plugs than setting off sparks? Gavin shows her the way, though, when he lets himself be charmed by the lady whose lips he yearns to kiss. Sandra has created a winner with this enthralling story.

In **SLOW BURN,** LOVESWEPT #547, by Cindy Gerard, passion heats to a boiling point between Joanna Taylor and Adam Dursky. When he takes on the job of handyman in her lodge, she's drawn to a loneliness in him that echoes her own, and she longs for his strong embrace with a fierce desire. Can a redheaded rebel who's given up on love heal the pain of a tough renegade? The intensity of Cindy's writing makes this a richly emotional tale you'll long remember.

In Linda Jenkins's newest LOVESWEPT, #548, Sam Wonder *is* **MR. WONDERFUL,** a heart-stopping combination of muscles and cool sophistication. But he's furious when Trina Bartok shows up at his Ozarks resort, convinced she's just the latest candidate in his father's endless matchmaking. Still, he can't deny the sensual current that crackles between them, and when Trina makes it clear she's there only for a temporary job, he resolves to make her a permanent part of his life. Be sure not to miss this treat from Linda.

Judy Gill's offering for the month, **SUMMER LOVER, LOVESWEPT #549,** will have you thinking summer may be the most romantic season of all—although romance is the furthest thing from Donna Mailer's mind when she goes to Gray Kincaid's office to refuse his offer to buy her uncle's failing campground business. After all, the Kincaid family nearly ruined her life. But Gray's passionate persuasion soon has her sweetly surrendering amid tangled sheets. Judy's handling of this story is nothing less than superb.

Most LOVESWEPTs end with the hero and heroine happily deciding to marry, but Olivia Rupprecht, who has quickly developed a reputation for daring to be different, begins **I DO!,** #550, with Sol Standish in the Middle East and Mariah Garnett in the Midwest exchanging wedding vows through the telephone—and that's before they ever lay eyes on each other. When they finally come face-to-face, will their innocent love survive the test of harsh reality? Olivia will take your breath away with this original and stunning romance.

INTIMATE VIEW by Diane Pershing, LOVESWEPT #551, will send you flying in a whirlwind of exquisite sensation. Ben Kane certainly feels that way when he glimpses a goddess rising naked from the ocean. He resented being in a small California town to run a cable franchise until he sees Nell Pritchard and she fires his blood—enough to make him risk the danger of pursuing the solitary spitfire whose sanctuary he's invaded. Diane's second LOVE-SWEPT proves she's one of the finest newcomers to the genre.

On sale this month from FANFARE are three marvelous novels. The historical romance **HEATHER AND VELVET** showcases the exciting talent of a rising star—Teresa Medeiros. Her marvelous touch for creating memorable characters and her exquisite feel for portraying passion and emotion shine in this grand adventure of love between a bookish orphan and a notorious highwayman known as the Dreadful Scot Bandit. Ranging from the storm-swept English countryside to the wild moors of Scotland, **HEATHER AND VELVET** has garnered the following praise from *New York Times* bestselling author Amanda Quick: "A terrific tale full of larger-than-life characters and thrilling romance." Teresa Medeiros—a name to watch for.

Lush, dramatic, and poignant, **LADY HELLFIRE**, by Suzanne Robinson, is an immensely thrilling historical romance. Its hero, Alexis de Granville, Marquess of Richfield, is a cold-blooded rogue whose tragic—and possibly violent—past has hardened his heart to love . . . until he melts at the fiery touch of Kate Grey's sensual embrace.

Anna Eberhardt, whose short romances have been published under the pseudonym Tiffany White, has been nominated for *Romantic Times*'s Career Achievement award for Most Sensual Romance in a series. Now she delivers **WHISPERED HEAT,** a compelling contemporary novel of love lost, then regained. When Slader Reems is freed after five years of being wrongly imprisoned, he sets out to reclaim everything that was taken from him—including Lissa Jamison.

Also on sale this month, in the Doubleday hardcover edition, is **LIGHTNING,** by critically acclaimed Patricia Potter. During the Civil War, nobody was a better Confederate blockade runner than Englishman Adrian Cabot, but Lauren Bradley swore to stop him. Together they would be swept into passion's treacherous sea, tasting deeply of ecstasy and the danger of war.

Happy reading!

With warmest wishes,

Nita Taublib
Associate Publisher
LOVESWEPT and FANFARE

FANFARE

FANFARE

Rosanne Bittner

_____ 28599-8 EMBERS OF THE HEART . $4.50/5.50 in Canada
_____ 29033-9 IN THE SHADOW OF THE MOUNTAINS
          $5.50/6.99 in Canada
_____ 28319-7 MONTANA WOMAN .... $4.50/5.50 in Canada
_____ 29014-2 SONG OF THE WOLF .... $4.99/5.99 in Canada

Deborah Smith

_____ 28759-1 THE BELOVED WOMAN .. $4.50/ 5.50 in Canada
_____ 29092-4 FOLLOW THE SUN .... $4.99/ 5.99 in Canada
_____ 29107-6 MIRACLE .... $4.50/ 5.50 in Canada

Tami Hoag

_____ 29053-3 MAGIC .... $3.99/4.99 in Canada

Dianne Edouard and Sandra Ware

_____ 28929-2 MORTAL SINS .... $4.99/5.99 in Canada

Kay Hooper

_____ 29256-0 THE MATCHMAKER, ... $4.50/5.50 in Canada
_____ 28953-5 STAR-CROSSED LOVERS .. $4.50/5.50 in Canada

Virginia Lynn

_____ 29257-9 CUTTER'S WOMAN, ... $4.50/4.50 in Canada
_____ 28622-6 RIVER'S DREAM, ... $3.95/4.95 in Canada

Patricia Potter

_____ 29071-1 LAWLESS .... $4.99/ 5.99 in Canada
_____ 29069-X RAINBOW .... $4.99/ 5.99 in Canada

Ask for these titles at your bookstore or use this page to order.

Please send me the books I have checked above. I am enclosing $ _____ (please add
$2.50 to cover postage and handling). Send check or money order, no cash or C. O. D.'s
please.

Mr./ Ms. _____

Address _____

City/ State/ Zip _____

Send order to: Bantam Books, Dept. FN, 414 East Golf Road, Des Plaines, IL 60016
Please allow four to six weeks for delivery.
Prices and availablity subject to change without notice.   FN 17 - 4/92